The Doll's House

KU-347-771

'Oh, wicked,' she sighed. It was a miniature house. She felt sure she'd seen it before. Then she realized it was one of those dream houses from inside her mind.

Becks, a rebellious young girl who won't go to school but dreams of her 'perfect house'; Patrick, a very ill teenager who has to stay in bed; Miss Amy Winters, an elderly spinster who looks back on her past and on a very special birthday present. Three very different people with something in common—the doll's house.

And then there are the dolls, who watch and wait but can never intervene.

Rachel Anderson was born in 1943 at Hampton Court. She and her husband, who teaches drama, have a daughter and three sons. She has worked in radio and newspaper journalism and in 1991 won the Medical Journalists' Association Award. She has written four books for adults, though now writes mostly for children. She won the Guardian Children's Fiction Award in 1992 for *Paper Faces*. When not writing, she is involved with the needs and care of children who are socially or mentally challenged.

Black Water

ISBN 0 19 271728 6

'This is a very sensitive and thought-provoking book which gives the reader an insight into what it must be like to suffer from epilepsy in the 1880s.' *In Brief*

'A rewarding and enriching reading experience for 12 to 14 year olds; it would be difficult to praise this book too highly.' *School Librarian*

The Working Class

ISBN 0 19 271717 0

'a sparky collection of linked short stories . . . inspired by first tastes of the world of work.' *Times Educational Supplement*

'the stories are funny, perceptive, compassionate and unsentimental.' *The Guardian*

Cover design by Slatter-Anderson
Cover illustration by Alan Fraser

WITHDRAWN

3300325446

The Doll's House

OXFORD BROOKES UNIVERSITY
LIBRARY   HARCOURT HILL

This book is to be returned on or before the last date stamped below.
A fine will levied on overdue books.
Books may be renewed by telephoning Oxford 488222
and quoting your borrower number.
You may not renew books that are reserved by another borrower.

06 APR 2001

1 7 MAR 2002

1 DEC 2004

2 3 MAR 2005

2 6 JAN 2006

1 4 NOV 2006

2 1 FEB 2007

2 2 OCT 2008

Other books by Rachel Anderson

The Poacher's Son
The War Orphan
French Lessons
The Bus People
Paper Faces
When Mum Went to Work
The Working Class
Black Water

For young readers

Little Angel Comes to Stay
Little Angel, Bonjour
Happy Christmas, Little Angel

Oxford Myths and Legends

Renard the Fox

The Doll's House

Rachel Anderson

Oxford University Press

Oxford New York Toronto

Oxford University Press, Walton Street, Oxford OX2 6DP

Oxford New York
Athens Auckland Bangkok Bombay
Calcutta Cape Town Dar es Salaam Delhi
Florence Hong Kong Istanbul Karachi
Kuala Lumpur Madras Madrid Melbourne
Mexico City Nairobi Paris Singapore
Taipei Tokyo Toronto

and associated companies in
Berlin Ibadan

Oxford is a trade mark of Oxford University Press

Text © Rachel Anderson 1995
First Published 1995

ISBN 0 19 271734 0

All rights reserved. No part of this publication may be
reproduced, stored in a retrieval system, or transmitted, in
any form or by any means, without the prior
permission in writing of Oxford University Press.
Within the U.K., exceptions are allowed in respect of
any fair dealing for the purpose of research or private
study, or criticism or review, as permitted under the
Copyright, Designs and Patents Act, 1988, or in the
case of reprographic reproduction in accordance
with the terms of the licences issued by the
Copyright Licensing Agency.
Enquiries concerning reproduction outside those terms
and in other countries should be sent to
the Rights Department, Oxford University Press,
at the address above.

A CIP catalogue record for this book is available
from the British Library

CLASS NO 823.9 0834 AND
ITEM NO 3300325446
THE LIBRARY
WESTMINSTER COLLEGE
OXFORD OX2 9AT

Printed and bound in Great Britain by
Biddles Ltd, Guildford and King's Lynn

PART ONE
Tuesday in the Morning

1 Catmeal Nuggets

Becks thought about kind houses. Welcoming, with friendly windows. Flowery curtains fluttered in the breeze. They had proper front doors, never locked but always open for running in and out any time you wanted. These houses had twisty wooden stairs that people could chase up and down, or just sit on and chat. They had warm wide kitchens, always set for tea with coloured check table-cloths and fruit-cake on a plate.

All Becks' houses in her mind were safe and sunny. Cheerful families lived and played together. There was no fighting in Becks' houses.

Becks lived with Sharon in Flat 43, on Level 5, of Block 4, on the Wellend Estate which was well-known for its goings-on. You could read about them in *The Courier* on Fridays. Sometimes there was even something about Wellend Estate on the telly, but only on local news.

Over on the other side of town, in a quiet tree-lined avenue called The Avenues, where sensible people lived with purpose and dignity in large villas, Patrick was thinking about sport. He thought about running without pain, about healthy lungs inhaling, strong thighs powering, nimble feet, winged as Hermes, flying over the springy turf. He thought about the cross-country the term they won. He thought about the Lake District last August when he and Dad set out early to conquer Hopegill Head.

And did.

Celebrating with cheese and chutney baps and ginger-beer shandy.

*　　*　　*

Miss Amy Winters thought about dear old Number Seven and the intricate delight that she and her childhood chums had had playing with it. She thought of the innumerable little people of subsequent generations who had also derived enjoyment from it.

She thought how strange it was that, despite a long and richly satisfying life in public service, both here and overseas, it should be a nursery doll's house put together by a jobbing carpenter over seven decades ago which predominantly preoccupied her of late.

Becks, shuffling disconsolately towards school, stopped thinking about beautiful houses and thought about bunking off.

Miss Amy Winters wondered how much longer before Number Seven might be returned to her. She wouldn't want to *play* with it. That would be absurd for a woman of seventy-nine. However, it would be so absolutely splendid to see it finally restored and ready for shipping out to Australia before she went to meet her Maker. She recalled its reassuring presence throughout her peaceful childhood, always there on the low table in the bay window of the nursery, ready to be played with.

She did so much hope that her second cousin's granddaughter in far-away Perth would welcome, enjoy, and cherish this gift which had been built for her own seventh birthday, a distant anniversary which now seemed quite close.

Patrick thought about whether the fizzing headache which began as he woke up was going to be one of the short ones or one of the long ones.

* * *

Miss Amy Winters wondered if it had, after all, been a sensible decision to let that poor sickly Chambers boy take responsibility for the reparations of Number Seven.

'Would we have been wiser, knowing that it is always easy to be wise after the event,' she turned and asked of her cat, 'to have sent it off to one of those specialist repairers who advertise in the county journals?'

'But no,' she replied on behalf of the cat. 'We both know we could never have afforded the prices that any skilled craftsman has to ask these days.'

At least the woodworm in the attic had been treated before it spread down into the bedrooms which was a mercy, and the boy had apparently begun seeing to the chimney stacks and those sadly broken banisters, though beyond that, he didn't seem to be making noticeable progress.

Perhaps it was not a suitable task for a boy. Yet surely it had been *his* idea to borrow it in the first place. Or was she misremembering? Was it in fact *she* who had forced the house upon the boy, who had been too polite or else too ill to resist? She knew that she could be more forceful than she intended. It had sometimes been a problem when handling younger members of staff.

Miss Amy Winters put her reflections about the doll's house aside, for they were proving negative and unprofitable.

'We will think only upon such things as are pure and of good repute, will we not?' she said to the cat. And she wondered instead about those new vegetarian catmeal nuggets she had seen advertised on the television just before the early evening news when they gave out that distressing item about the wave of muggings on the Wellend Estate.

'We'll give the new nuggets a try, shall we, old thing?'

Becks thought some more about bunking off. If only it'd still been pissing down, and if only her tacky trainers and her yukky nylon anorak what Sharon got cheap off the charity

5

shop had been letting in the rain, then she'd have given the bunk-off a miss. On wet days you got loads of attention. The school secretary let you dry off beside the radiator in her office.

But no rain. Dry, bright, and breezy. A fine yes-day to find out if she had the bottle to do a bunk. But she better make up her mind p.d.q. She was nearly at the crossing. She could see the lollipop lady striding out on to the zebra with her lemon-yellow stick and big fluorescent gloves. Even from a distance, that lady glowed. And she had the power. And she was strong. And she was kind to people.

With just a flick of that slender STOP-stick, she made a mammoth truck, filled to the brim with mashed-up cars going off to the grinder, screech to a halt. Then the little children trotted safely over to the other side.

The lollipop lady knew every child by sight and many by name as well.

On days when Becks was glum and hungry, the glowing lady found her something to eat in her yellow pocket. She didn't do that to all the children. Perhaps she could tell which ones didn't get breakfast.

Still, one kind lollipop lady, who knew your name and sometimes found a fluffy toffee to see you through the morning, was no excuse for wimping out. Becks had to bunk off now, quick, before she was dragged along by a surge of mums and buggies.

She checked it was safe behind, none of the Class 6 bully boys sneaking up. Then she turned and skimmed quickly past the boarded-up betting shop, past *New Waves*, past the boarded-up hairdresser's, past the off-licence so thick with metal grills it looked as though it was closed even when it wasn't. Round here, nobody trusted anybody.

Then, quick as one of them nits that Mrs Whitton said jumped from one head to the next if you didn't keep your hair tidy, Becks hopped sideways down the dark alley between the boarded-up greengrocer's and the used-clothes charity shop till she was flitting, free as a flea on a rat, along the foot-path down to the allotments.

Most days, you felt like you were one of them slugs Miss brought in for the Alive to Nature Week. But just some days, like today, you knew you could fly if you were given half a chance.

'No one never gives me a quarter a chance of nothing,' she said. It was something Sharon used to say. 'So if they don't give it me, I gotta get it myself.' Sharon said that too, to explain when she'd nicked something.

Becks began to skip. And she felt like she was flying.

Patrick watched the ceiling. It was high and ornate with greyish-white foliage arranged in a formal circle around the central light fixture. It was the dining-room ceiling. These days, he had to have his bed on the ground floor.

He resigned himself with great reluctance to another day at home, for he was as invertebrate as a slug. And slugs did not attend school. He was as cold-blooded as a slug, too. Even under the 15-tog duvet the tips of his fingers remained bloodlessly yellow and unfeeling with cold.

At least slugs could get out and about by themselves. Indeed, the speed of racing slugs under rugged playground conditions, as he recalled from last term, was surprisingly fast.

This morning, Patrick felt he could scarcely sit up unaided. As he waited for his mother, he moved his gaze slowly, for even rotating his eyes was painful, from the dusty ceiling leaves to the decorative marble mantelpiece, then to his uniform hanging on the back of the chair like a limp headless scholar. It was purple, with gold stripes on the tie and on the crest on the blazer pocket; not real gold, more margarine yellow which they referred to as 'gold' at the school outfitter's. Anybody seeing the purple and gold recognized it at once as the colours of the Boys' High, a demanding academic institution for the bright-eyed sons of lawyers and doctors who would themselves one day turn into keen medics and QCs. Patrick left his uniform out on the chair as an emblem of hope to himself.

His mother came in and heaved him upright, then plumped up the pillows behind him. He felt he was becoming like one of those smelly drunks who slumped their days away in the ring-road underpass. She handed him his breakfast drink and hovered nearby in case he lost his grip and dropped it. At least drunks could grab a bottle, raise it to their lips and find oblivion.

'It's banana, dear.' It was liquidized to a nourishing mush in goats' milk. There was supposed to be something about goats' milk which was better for you than cows' milk. 'I put in a pinch of ginger to liven it up, all right?'

Patrick nodded, drank, sighed. Even slugs were allowed to sigh.

'Cheer up, old bean,' his mother said, too brightly. 'You can't go in this week so there's no use going on about it.'

He wasn't going on. It was strange that she should even think he was. He'd have liked to argue, sulk like teenage sons were supposed to, but invertebrates don't go on about things.

He wondered if the plaster rose-leaves had been made from a mould or modelled by a craftsman's hand.

'Perhaps next week you'll make it,' she said, always optimistic. Surely she and Dad must have realized by now that he was likely to get a lot worse before he began to get better? So why did she persist with her relentless good cheer?

'And try and do something about your lunch today, won't you? Just a bit? If only to please Mrs Murphy.'

He nodded. Next week the other boys started Trials. He had to be there. If he couldn't sit exams with the rest of them he'd be done for.

'Thanks, Mum,' he said. She kissed his forehead and went off to get herself ready for work. Busy, busy slug's mum.

2 Cheese and Pickle

There were people out on the allotments. The fine morning had lured them down from the Blocks. Becks hadn't expected people. It turned out to be a naff place for a kid to hang out anyway. You were too visible. It was like a wide open plain. As she went bob-bob-bobbing like a robin between the hedges and the strips of corrugated iron that made up the fences she kept meeting men.

First it was an old geezer walking a dog. A crusty old geezer of a dog, too. Dog and man both had gluey eyes. Becks didn't go for dogs. The dog stopped walking and growled at Becks' trainers, then changed direction and sniffed out rubbish stuck in the hedge while the old man glared at Becks.

'You not got nothing better to do than gawp?' Becks snapped. 'And another thing. You old people didn't ought to be allowed to keep dogs in the flats. It's not natural.' She knew why they did it though. Because some nights they were scared witless by the noisy goings-on in the stairwells.

Further on were more men doing things to the earth in their plots. Every single one gave Becks the evil eye. People were suspicious of kids, specially round here where they were usually up to no good and you only got to know about it afterwards in *The Courier*.

Becks hadn't done anything yet. But she felt that soon she would have, once she'd decided what it was. Meanwhile, you had to keep walking. Had to look as though you were going somewhere. It was the loitering they didn't like.

Patrick wanted to take hold of his soul, buried so deeply in his soft slug's body that he could hardly feel it, and to shake it till it responded and kick-started back into life.

Now listen here, old soul, he spoke firmly. You are better off than many. People do not die of an immune dysfunction. They struggle to overcome its innumerable symptoms and pains. They endure it for maybe two, five, ten, or fifteen years. Twenty per cent recover completely. Many recover quite a lot. And there is no recorded evidence that people die of it.

Patrick considered that the one way he might die would be by suicide but that, as Father O'Brien had chosen to remind him, was a mortal sin. And unless things got very, very much worse, Patrick knew he was unlikely to follow that particular path to eternal damnation because of the immense anguish it would cause his parents who, in their own ineffectual, hopelessly crushing and demanding way, loved him and were endeavouring to do the best for him.

Suddenly, unexpectedly, Becks came upon a perfect little house just by the hedge full of rubbish. It wasn't *quite* like the one in her head, but near enough. It had that friendly open look that made it seem as though it was welcoming her in.

It was mostly made of wood, with a sloping roof, a wide window at the front, and a row of sturdy red tulips growing round the door, just like a real picture-book house should have. A person could tie some pretty cloth over the window like curtains and live there forever, safe and snug and far from that nagging hag called Sharon.

The door stood open, as though waiting for her, or some other child very like her, to wander in. There was no one about. Becks went up the two steps.

Inside wasn't so good, not a dream home at all, just a shed made of old doors nailed together, and filled with clutter. It didn't have any little twisty wooden stairs. There wasn't a fire-place, nor a kitchen table laid for tea on a check cloth with a warm smell of baked cake and happiness.

There was just a broken canvas chair, a wobbly old table with tools on it, and a smell of earth and damp.

Tools and gardening things took up most of the space, though if you had to live here, you could get rid of them easy enough, go down the second-hand shop, end of Grimsy Street. With the money you could buy yourself a tin cup, a sleeping-bag, and some chocolate, just like Dean's brother did. When he was on the run, he found himself a portable telephone someone had left lying around just inside an open window. He sold it to the second-hand shop down the Grimsy Road, bought himself the sleeping-bag and food, and lived rough for nearly a week before they got him.

But Dean's brother was thirteen, looked fifteen and he was a boy. Boys were lucky. People took notice of boys. Boys could always do things. People always wanted boys. Sharon said she'd wanted a boy, too.

'And look what I got! You.'

Becks tried the pockets of a man's jacket hanging on a nail on the wall. In one, a sandwich in a brown paper bag, cheese and Branston pickle. Pity about the pickle. In the other, a five pence piece. Hardly worth the effort. But she took it anyway, along with the sandwich, before slipping outside.

Like Dean said, nicking small stuff didn't count. If they had it, and you needed it, and they weren't even using it, then it was OK to help yourself. You were liberating it to benefit the poor, like Robin Hood.

'Oi!'

Becks dropped down behind a plastic water butt. She wasn't quick enough.

'Oi, you!' It was one of those men working over on his plot. He'd stopped his hoeing. He was watching her.

'Oi, you over there!' he called again.

Becks took no notice.

The fellow put down his hoe. He strode along the grassy bits between the plots like he thought he was head of the police informer's club.

'Oi! Come on, you!'

Thinks I'm afraid of him, Becks thought. I'll kill him first.

The men round here did quite different things from the women. Men got into arguments, hung around, yelled at people, while the women mostly got on with doing useful things and being busy, like Mrs Ahmed who came into school Wednesdays to help with Read Aloud afternoons, like the lollipop lady who helped people not to get run over by the trucks, like the school secretary who helped you dry out on wet days, like Mrs Whitton. All except for Sharon who hung around doing nothing except for shouting at people just like the men.

'My name's not Oi,' Becks called back.

'Never mind that. Out of here, you.' He shook his fist.

Becks hated it when people shouted at her. It made her go trembly inside. 'Not doing nothing. Why pick on me?'

'Some story! Get on with you.' He was angry. Answering back made him angrier. 'What you doing round here anyway? You ought to be in school.'

'What's it to you? Anyway, we got the day off. Staff training.'

'What's your name?'

'None of your business. And if you dare touch me I'll do you for assault.' Or maybe not, thought Becks.

He withdrew his hand. Awesome how jittery some of them were when you got close to. But he wouldn't leave off yelling at her, standing there with his big white arms beside a row of green sprouting plants as though the whole world was his.

'You're a thieving little tyke. You was round here last week, wasn't you?'

'No,' said Becks. 'Never been here before in my life.'

It wasn't fair. You got told off whether or not you did something.

'Yes you was and picked all my onions.'

Onions? Who'd want to pick someone's onions. 'You're barmy,' she said. 'I can't stand onions.'

'Listen, you. None of us on the Allotment Society want you kids hanging round here. You're just a menace. No sense of decency, any of you. Come round just looking for trouble, don't you?'

'OK, cool it, Mister Muscleman,' said Becks. 'I'm off.

Watch me vanish.' Moving her legs specially slowly as though she had to drag them behind her, she left. She could feel his eyes in her back watching her all the way.

Pity about the shed. It would've been brilliant if it had turned out right, with flowery curtains already at the window and a check cloth and a fruit-cake on the table. If that'd been her home, she'd have got a kitten to come and live there with her and made it into her friend.

One day she'd find that house of her own. And when she did, she'd never in a million years tell Sharon where it was so Sharon wouldn't even be able to write to her.

If only you were allowed to choose yourself a new mother that'd be ace. And if you were, Becks reckoned she'd probably choose the lollipop lady.

Miss Amy Winters said goodbye to Marmalade and set out with her purse and her bag of old bread to walk to the residents' park at the end of The Avenues. Overhead, the high scudding clouds in the golden sky filled her with much joy. She would definitely buy some of those new nuggets on the way home for Marmalade to try.

Meanwhile, she would endeavour not to worry about Number Seven for, as everybody knew, empty worry just breeds disease.

13

3 Jelly Babies

Becks found the path that led to the footbridge over the railway. She heard the train coming and raced up the clanky metal steps so she'd be on top, dead centre, when it streaked under.

It was an InterCity, eleven coaches long. The metal plates rattled under her feet and hot rubbery air whooshed up into her face. Becks giggled. It was like being Concorde, flying.

This bridge was a grand place. Boys from the estate used to hang out here. Last August, one of them from school tossed a great block of wood down on to the rails. But some creep had seen it and rang through to the railway police. People said it was one of the Ahmed brothers, always grassing. All the trains got stopped and there were police everywhere for days.

They did all sorts on the estate. Thieving, firing, cars, assault. Younger kids mostly stuck with the light stuff. A bit of nicking and pocket-dipping. They did it off each other, too, which Becks reckoned was stupid, specially after someone nicked her trainers which weren't even new. They ought to broaden out.

She unwrapped the hoe-man's cheese sandwich and picked out the onion pickle with her little pinky finger. She really hated pickle.

If Sharon ever bothered to make Becks a sandwich for her dinner, which was so rare you had to applaud, she larded it with pickle just for spite.

After the sandwich, Becks looked for something to throw. But they must have cleaned up since Dean found that great railway sleeper and lugged it on to the bridge. Becks tossed the brown paper bag. It flapped like a bird, then fell. No fun.

When the police got hold of Dean, they asked him why he'd done it.

'To see what would happen, a course. Why d'you think? There's nothing else to do round here.'

Becks heard them in the secretary's office talking about Dean. The lollipop lady said they should've asked Dean a few questions *before* he did it. Then they might have had the foresight to find him something more useful to do than chucking timber about. Mrs Whitton had agreed that it would've saved them a load of trouble.

Dean got sent away to a special school. They only let him come back sometimes. Becks wished she'd get sent away.

All of a sudden it was naff standing on a stupid bridge waiting for a stupid train. Becks wished she was inside one of her dream houses, lying under a cosy blanket, watching the bright cotton curtains flutter at the friendly windows, waiting for tea.

She went down on to the line and thought about putting the five pence piece on the rail so it'd turn into a ten pence when the wheels ran over it. But it wasn't worth the bother. Ten pence was nearly as useless as five.

Becks reckoned that if she could find her way to Town, she'd try a bit of dipping out there. Even if she never got anything, at least it would make her bunk-off worth talking about tomorrow.

She'd been to Town before when Mrs Whitton took the class to see costumes of old-fashioned people in the Civic Museum. They went in a special school coach.

McDonald's was in Town, and the Mall with the lottery ticket seller and the buskers hanging round with their music and manky dogs on strings. There'd be the sickly petal smell from the hand-made soap shop, and the sickly sugar smell from the Pick 'n' Mix Sweetie Stall. The people were so greedy about getting their Pick 'n' Mix into the bag, they dropped sweets all over the ground and you could gather them up.

Oh yes, even if you only had five pee, going into Town would be ace.

There was supposed to be a short cut over the other side of the footbridge. It saved you using the bus, so Karen's big sister said. But going down the steps on the far side of the footbridge was like stepping off the edge of the world. She was into No-Go land. Becks had never been to Town on her own. She didn't know the way.

Patrick shifted cautiously. It hurt. His legs, his back. Not so bad you'd cry out. Not like a kick in the shins on the football pitch. Oh, for the joy of *that* kind of pain. An injury inflicted in the heat of the match. This was slow spasmodic pain which came and went, and on and on, and you didn't know, nobody knew, how long it was going to last and when it was going to start getting better.

There were good days when you woke feeling as zesty as a fresh lemon. But that only served to remind you with fearful irony what life could be like when there was no sapping of energy, no confusion. When all that seeped back an hour later, the loss was crucial.

At the onset of the disease, Father O'Brien had called and reminded him he should continue to pray.

Miss Hoppy from next door also dropped by and suggested that Patrick might like to try writing some poetry about his sufferings so that, when he was strong again, he could join her Neighbourhood Poetry Circle. And the ancient woman from down the far end of The Avenues, who his mother was friendly with, arranged for him to have her old toy house brought round. She'd reminded him, rather firmly, of his offer to mend some of the fiddly carpentry bits on the roof. But that had been ages ago when this thing had only just begun and he was able to go to school most days. No one then had any idea how it was going to drag on. They thought it was just the flu.

His three best friends from the High still occasionally dropped by with some of his homework, but only when they wanted help with their own. Patrick used to get straight A's.

Gradually, all of them lost interest as he failed, with extreme lack of drama, to get better.

These days, I'm nothing but a corpse with a living head, Patrick thought.

* * *

16

Becks criss-crossed an industrial estate. It had nice pavements, neat roads, lamp-posts, all there for nobody. It wasn't alive with thieving and fighting and people like on Wellend. It was all closed up, warehouses and carpet showrooms all abandoned. Further on, there were high wire fences with security arc-lights fixed up and scary black pictures of fierce dogs' heads with snarling lips.

It didn't look right. There ought to be a McDonald's soon, and bustle, and the ground ought to be covered in sweeties.

The other time she'd been to Town was with Nasreen and her mum. They took her to look at the Christmas decorations when the new Mall opened. Nasreen's family didn't go in for Christmas, but Mrs Ahmed said there was nothing in anybody's holy book to stop them enjoying the pretty lights.

They'd gone on a bus. Becks didn't know which one.

When they'd got to the Pick 'n' Mix Sweetie Stall with its sugary smell, Mrs Ahmed had laughed out loud and clapped her hands together so that her bracelets tinkled like Christmas bells.

'This is taking me right back to Bengali Sweet Market when I was small.' She was so happy to be remembering it that she bought a bag of black and yellow jelly babies for Nasreen and Becks to share. Nasreen never minded sharing.

All afternoon Mrs Ahmed held them kindly by their hands so they wouldn't get lost in the crowd. She let them look at all the toys in all the shops and never once told them to hurry up. She made it seem like she had all day just for them. Then she took them to the *It's the Real Thing!* ice-cream parlour. They sat on high stools with long shiny legs like magic insects. She bought them ice-cream sundaes with paper umbrellas. She had a glass of cold tea. She said, 'And this reminds me of the hot season when I was a small girl. All my aunties drank iced tea in those days. Now they just want fizzy drinks.'

The only time she'd been upset was when they'd seen the buskers. Mrs Ahmed had been shocked at the busker girls' tacky clothing. But she'd given them money anyway.

17

'Oh, but always it is such a blessing to give to the visibly poor,' she said smiling.

Sharon never gave anything to anybody. She said buskers were all hopheads and scum of the earth.

Before they came home, Mrs Ahmed took them to McDonald's. She didn't buy burgers because Nasreen's family didn't go in for eating cows. She got them each a mega portion of chips.

Afterwards, Becks told Sharon that if you were allowed to choose your own mother, she'd choose Mrs Ahmed. And Sharon replied, 'That's the last time I let you go prancing off with that Mrs Whatsername. Just spoiled you something rotten. No wonder you're such a pest. I already had a letter from school about you. So you watch it, my girl.'

Becks hadn't been to Town since.

'You been pestering me over that ever since your so-called friends took you down there,' Sharon said. 'Well, no is no.'

Saturdays, when Sharon might've taken her, she said she was tired.

'You try bringing up a kid like you in a muck-heap like this. You'll soon learn what tired means.'

Never too tired to go dancing down the *Florida* club Saturday nights, Becks noticed.

After the move to the dining-room, Patrick's mother suggested bringing the television in.

'No thanks, Mum.'

Watching family game-shows and afternoon films which were made before even his parents were born made the loneliness worse. Some days his sight was bad so he couldn't focus properly on the screen. Other times it was the concentration which failed and he couldn't follow even the silliest sitcom re-run.

Patrick closed his eyes and listened to the radio. He had it on very softly for the sound aggravated the tinnitus in his ears, though today that wasn't so bad.

Patrick was half listening to an interview with a feminist

explorer. Oh, most fortunate female, who had the stamina to brave those leeches, poisoned arrows, sheer cliff climbs, sweltering nights in the bush. Would that he too, mere male, could be pitting his body against the physical dangers of the world.

And after her, the cricket. Would he ever again grasp the willow?

Would anything ever happen to him again between now and old age?

Becks walked forever, till her knees were aching, till she was so hungry she felt she could probably eat frittered ratburger, so long as it came with chips. That's what she'd once told Arnie she'd eaten. That bad bully even believed her.

And still she hadn't found the way to Town. When you thought about it, with the shop counters loaded with bright pretty things waiting for you to help yourself, and the smell of chips frying and scented bath oils inside your head, Town was near. When you tried to get to it, it slunk itself away out of reach.

4 Curdled Eggs

Patrick heard the click of the back door. The cleaning woman letting herself in.

Mrs Murphy came with a keen recommendation from Father O'Brien as being urgently in need of work. Even so, Patrick's mother's vaguely liberal, egalitarian tendencies caused her a certain amount of disquiet about employing someone less educated, less skilled, less well off than herself to come in and see to the domestic toil while she herself was at liberty to do stimulating and enjoyable work in the pleasant, well-appointed Social Advice Bureau, for which she was trained and well-paid.

Patrick's father, whose main job, as far as Patrick could make out, was to sit scheming in his F.E. college of one hundred and one ways to overthrow the Principal, had no such half-hearted prickings of conscience regarding Mrs Murphy for he seldom had cause to see her.

Patrick was concerned about Mrs Murphy's employment within his family, though not in the same way as his mother. He felt an increasing irritation that she should be there at all.

Lonely and abandoned by his friends, he resented the fact that the only regular company now available to him was a hired scrubber off the Wellend Estate. Patrick suspected that the woman's very presence in his home was a hindrance to recovery. And she smelled terrible, like a walking ashtray. Even when she wasn't lounging about in the kitchen smoking and drinking tea, she wasn't efficient. Every task Mrs Murphy undertook she performed to the worst of her ability. She was supposed to prepare him a light lunch from ingredients bought and put ready in the fridge by Patrick's mother. On the advice of the medical centre's dietician, Patrick was now on a dairy-product-free, sugar-free diet. Mrs Murphy did not hold with this. She believed in eggs.

20

'No wonder you aren't getting well if you aren't eating your eggs,' she told Patrick. If there was enough goodness in an egg, she explained, for creating a whole new hen, then there was enough to make a sickly boy well.

The sulphuric smell and rubbery texture of a boiled egg made Patrick nauseous.

'Scrambled then. With toast. That's invalid food if ever there was.'

She ignored the tofu squares, the yeast-free oatcakes, the organically grown, pesticide-free fresh fruit, put ready for Patrick's lunch, and instead selected and ruined two eggs and an ordinary slice of bread with her version of scrambling and toasting. One time Patrick actually saw the cigarette ash on the edge of the plate.

As she stumbled in with the plate, she expressed surprise that he wasn't getting better, as though it was his own fault.

'By your age all my six boys was off on their apprenticeships. Even them that couldn't find work, they were off doing odd jobs. Not taking it easy on their backsides. Though I dare say it stops that bed floating away if you keep laying on it like that. That's useful in itself.'

Some days, Patrick desperately wanted to explain to her about the chronic nature and likely prognosis of this viral infection. One time he had even got as far as patiently explaining to her how it represses the immune system a bit like Aids. 'Except of course it's not Aids,' he'd quickly added but then saw that she wasn't even listening.

Today he didn't feel strong enough to explain anything. So he listened to her prejudiced mouth-noise flowing into his ears. At least it drowned the other aural disturbances which were inside his head.

'So, as I told my brother-in-law, with that Father O'Brien almost begging me to help your mother out, what was I to do? And just so long as there's no infection involved, then I'm happy to keep coming. But this is a funny old household, to be sure.'

Patrick looked at the curdled eggs which Mrs Murphy had so painstakingly ruined.

'Thank you, Mrs Murphy,' he said.

'Anything else now, Patsy?'

He wished she wouldn't call him that.

'You need help with that other little thing?'

Patrick shook his head.

Mrs Murphy's other claim to usefulness was that she was supposed, when his legs were very painful and he could hardly walk, to help him to the w.c., not the upstairs bathroom, just along the hall to the downstairs toilet.

'And only if he asks,' Patrick's mother had stressed in a quiet voice.

Never would Patrick be asking for that favour, not even if Mrs Murphy wore a blindfold and were deaf and dumb. He'd rather hold on till his father got back, or else die of kidney stones. Even having his mother help was tricksy.

He heard the click of the back door as Mrs Murphy, no doubt well pleased with her achievements with two eggs, some cigarette ash, and a can of spray-on furniture polish, departed.

In solitude, Patrick dozed. It was encouraging that his spine had stopped hurting so much.

5 Soggy Bread in Water

What a naffhead! She'd ended up in the wrong place, over where the hincty folks lived.

Becks could tell. These were poshos all right. Each house stood alone in a garden all its own. Their grass was green. Their trees still had branches.

Round Wellend, the nearest thing to a garden was the scabby patch just outside each block, crumbly with dog dirt. Last year three trees got planted. Their branches got pulled off and they were dead now. There weren't flowerbeds up Wellend either, just a patch of coloured crisp packets round the bottom of the three dead trees.

Becks jumped to grab a low-hanging branch with both hands. She dragged on it till it tore away with a creaking noise. It sounded good.

I'm going to zap these people and grieve them till they're begging me for mercy. That was something Mikey in Class 6 used to say. Becks thought it was ace the way he said it.

With the branch, she swiped at the pink blossoms on the flowering trees in the rich gardens. She made it snow rosy snow all along their tidy pavement.

As if their gardens weren't enough for them, they had a park too, surrounded by black-painted iron railings. Up Wellend the nearest thing to a park was two kiddy swings which hadn't got seats any more. The loose metal chains dangled down and clanked in the wind.

FOR RESIDENTS' USE ONLY, said a sign at the entrance, so Becks went in. She was waiting to be yelled at to get out. She had her smart answer all ready.

But nobody took any notice. Could be posh people had other ways than yelling.

Inside the residents' park there were more notices.

NO BALL GAMES TO BE PLAYED, said one.

Becks wished she'd got a football, then she'd kick it and wham it till it scuffed their fancy grass, smacked into their plants, till they got livid.

Another sign by their swings, which still had seats, said:

No children under 12 admitted without accompanying adult. No children over 12 to play on apparatus.

Becks had no accompanying adult. Yet no one accosted her as she swung and swung, higher and higher.

A third notice said:

Due to Misuse, These Public Toilets to be Closed, as from 13 April. Nearest Public Conveniences Situated on Mandesley Road.

Becks was surprised that posh people would misuse toilets. She thought it was only rough slags like Craig's and Warren's dads who smashed up toilets when they felt bad.

There was a pond in the park. That had a notice too.

DO NOT FEED THE WILDFOWL. Becks had nothing to feed them with.

At school, they said Becks couldn't read. They sent her to the dappy reading unit once a week. But she could read notices like these well enough. Any dum-dum could.

Plain as could be it said *not* to feed the fowl. And there sat an old biddy filling the pond with great crusts of bread which were floating around in soggy swollen gobbets.

Miss Amy Winters settled on a bench in the park to feed the birds and to count her many blessings.

The warm sun on her back. Alive to another spring. Old legs that hadn't seized up. An adequate pension. All her paperwork, bills and wills, seen to so that when she passed on, she'd cause no trouble to anybody, least of all her second cousin's son in Perth. The affection of a loyal cat. Memories of a peaceful childhood.

When she opened the plastic bag, a flurry of ducks and geese, pigeons and sparrows, surrounded her eagerly. She threw them their bread, piece by piece.

She was lifted down from her perambulator by her

24

nursemaid in order to feed the ducks like this nearly a lifetime ago.

She watched a small child over on the swings. When one was no longer so active oneself, it was a pleasure to see others at play.

Miss Amy Winters noticed the child leave the swings, and wander off to admire the flowerbeds, so glorious now with golden daffs set off by white hyacinths.

But, oh no, how *most* unfortunate. The child was *not* admiring, but swiping with a stick. Then, rapidly tiring of that fruitless occupation, he or she wandered disconsolately towards the pond. It looked such a vulnerable young thing, but looks could deceive and the mother of mischief is no bigger than a midge's wing. As the child approached, Miss Winters saw how pale and dirty its face was. And it was scowling.

Miss Winters was about to remonstrate, quite gently, about the sadness of knocking off the flower heads when the child spoke.

'What was that, dear?' said Miss Winters.

'I said,' snarled the child, sitting down on the bench beside her, 'can't you read, lady, or what? It says *don't* feed them ducks, up there. Look.'

'Yes, dear, I know. But the ducks do so enjoy a treat. It's only a little I'm giving them. The breeding season makes them extra hungry.'

The child said something that sounded like, 'Silly old bag.'

Miss Amy Winters patted the bench beside her, encouraging the child to join her in feeding the birds. The child hesitated a moment, then changed its mind and moved much closer. The child accepted the bread Miss Winters held out, threw the whole piece at a pigeon which fluttered up in alarm, then suddenly rose and ran off in a sulk.

How upsetting it all was. Children these days just didn't appear to enjoy the same innocent contentment as those of earlier generations. Still, better to dwell on the positive rather than the negative. At least the behaviour of ducks and geese had not altered in the passage of time.

When, half an hour later, Miss Winters left the bench to

proceed to the shops for her paper and the nuggets she discovered that her purse had gone. The first reaction was confusion. She had definitely had it here with her. Then dismay at the loss. Then renewed sorrow at the state of modern childhood.

Then remorse that she was partly to blame. She should have taken more care. After all, it is opportunity which makes the thief.

What had she lost? One pound and sixty pence, her Senior Citizen's bus pass, her Pension Book, and a blurred photograph of Marmalade.

Nothing she could do about it now of course, except tell Marmalade. And at least she hadn't been mugged as well. That was worth rejoicing over. And it was a poor heart that never rejoiced.

6 Doggy in the Dining-room

The cheese sarnie was a lifetime back. Weird how a hungry stomach kept speaking to you. Must be nearly dinnertime. In class, they'd be getting ready. If only she was back there now. She could sneak out to the cloakroom and take first pick round the other people's dinner bags.

At least she'd got some money. Nearly two quid. Shame was, there weren't any shops. Posh people all go shopping with their chauffeurs.

The houses by the park had driveways. Becks chose the one with an overgrown garden and stone lions up on the gateposts for its garage stood open and there were no cars inside. That meant they'd gone out.

She skittled along the edge of the drive, sliding between the shaggy bushes, up the front steps. She knew she was a mean cool dealer in dodgery. She peered through the letter-box.

No noises. Not a lot to see inside. A tiled floor, shiny with polish, a WELCOME doormat, letters on a table. Then she saw the guard dog come padding into view.

People on the estate went in for dogs. They barked all night and bit by day. Some people, specially the ones who got themselves a dog, said you needed them to defend yourself against riff-raff and scum.

This dog was low and hairy. It glared at Becks as she peered through the letter-box. It opened its mouth, all drippy wet, showing its yellow teeth. Becks was going to scram quick. Then she saw it was smiling at her. It looked just like that old biddy opposite, in flat 42, when she got her new set of dentures. The first decent smile Becks had had from anyone all day. Smiled at by a dog. This was a yes day.

'Bog off, then, dog,' Becks hissed.

The dog wagged its tail and waddled out of view.

Patrick woke to hear his grandfather's grandfather clock in the hall chiming the half-hour. He dozed and woke through much of each day. It never made him rested. When his mother returned, she would help him do his stretching exercises which prevented muscle-wasting. Now he wondered, alarmed, if hallucinations were another part of the disorder for, outside the window, in amongst the straggling clematis creeper, he seemed to have seen the fleeting face of the wild Green Man.

Out there below the dining-room window was a sour sunless place for shrubs. His father wanted to cut them back. Patrick claimed he liked them that way. It offered a small world for him to view from the bed, of spiders spinning webs, blue tits hopping feverishly from twig to twig, the slow progress of an emerald caterpillar up a stalk. Even the greenfly were entertainment, while demanding nothing from him, not even his recovery.

Now here was something new, a pointy elfin countenance, framed in leaves, a face so pale it was almost green. Perhaps a visual disturbance. And if hallucinations were not part of the disorder, he'd know he was indeed turning into a basket case.

There were already so many symptoms. The pain in the limbs, the nausea, the low fevers, the palpitations, brightness of the light, the awful distortions of sound like rushing waterfalls inside the ears which would not cease their roaring and cascading, and blocking out all other sounds.

The GP had asked him to describe it.

'It's not actually like anything I've ever experienced,' Patrick said wearily, for these repeated visits to the surgery exhausted him. 'So I can't really say what it's like.'

'Try,' urged the doctor, glancing at his watch and smiling across at Patrick's mother in a patronizing way. 'Do your best.'

At every consultation Patrick had the impression that the doctor didn't believe any of this really mattered.

'Well, I suppose,' Patrick began uncertainly, 'the nearest I can come to it is saying it's like having a lavatory cistern stuck inside my skull which keeps flushing automatically every few seconds and won't ever stop.'

The doctor smirked. 'Glad he hasn't lost his humour, anyway!'

I'm not trying to be funny, Patrick thought. None of this is funny. The edge to the man's laughter had set off the noise again.

'Some nights it's so screechy it wakes me. Other times, it seems to be set off by ordinary sounds.'

'Tinnitus,' the doctor said, smiling. 'Just another manifestation of his still mysterious syndrome.' He spoke to Patrick's mother as though Patrick weren't there. 'If indeed this is one of the chronic fatigue syndromes that is presenting, or another post-viral condition. We can't let it drag on forever. I suppose we'd better put him down for a referral to the consultant.'

He scribbled importantly on a pad of paper.

'As for the tinnitus, not a lot we can do about it, but you could try giving him another sound-source, to mask the irritation. A radio, on a low volume. Some sufferers find it helps.'

A radio, Patrick thought? Is that all you can prescribe? Just supposing I don't *want* to listen to the radio night and day?

Patrick's mother nodded eagerly.

'At least you can take comfort, old chap,' said the doctor speaking specially loudly as though he believed that Patrick was deaf and stupid as well as sick, 'in the knowledge that nobody *ever* died of a noise in the ears!'

It was meant to be more humour.

On reaching home, Miss Amy Winters consoled, and was consoled by, the cat.

'So I'm sorry, my dear, but I was unable to buy you those nuggets,' she explained softly, 'as I no longer have my purse.'

Better by far to reveal her sad secrets to Marmalade than tell them to someone who might misconstrue them and pass them on.

The trouble with theft was that, all too often, it released so many other bad feelings which spread out like the dark ink of the squid, shadowing the brighter aspects of life.

It was neat trying to get into houses when the people weren't there. You could imagine how it'd be if you lived there instead. Last week, Ma McEwans, the old biddy across the landing in flat 42 forgot to slam her door properly. So Becks went in. She poked around in Ma McEwans's kitchen, looked in the drawers, all stuffed with used plastic bags, then in the wardrobe. Full of old pink underwear and yellow vests. And under the bed. Nothing but knobbly old shoes covered with dust.

So Becks didn't take anything. Nothing worth taking, not even bingo money in a jar.

Poor old hinny living all alone and no one ever visiting. Her six grandsons were all doing time, that's what Sharon claimed, and her daughter-in-law never bothering with her even though she was only over on Block 6.

A dry branch poked Becks in the cheek. These posh people ought to see to their gardens. It was a struggle getting through the bushes to the next window. The windowsill was too high. Becks wasn't big. She wasn't strong either, though she let it be known at school that she worked out in a gym. She had to heave herself up on her arms. It hurt.

But it was worth it. She saw into a lovely sitting-room, just like in Sharon's shopping catalogue, two deep settees, pink velvet covers, armchairs matching. There was a jar of flowers on a piano. Next window along, she saw a serious room, nothing but books, books, books right up to the ceiling. Dread, dread. No rooms like that in the catalogue. Looked more like the public library.

The next one was dark, with a fire-place up one end. You could have lit a real fire in it, like in the olden days. But the grate was empty except for a half-moon of paper folded like a fan. Down the middle of the room stood a heavy polished table with chairs round it. There were brown paintings with carved frames on the walls, like the pictures they'd seen in the City Museum. In the olden days, and in places like the Mayor's house, people had a special room, separate from where they did the cooking, just for sitting down and eating their dinner, that's what Miss said.

Back in Flat 43, Sharon didn't have a table with chairs all round. Becks had her tea off her knee in front of the telly. Sharon took hers leaning up against the kitchen drainer so she'd be handy for the sink for flicking her ash.

Becks was just going to move off when she caught sight of something awesome standing in the shadows of the room.

'Oh, wicked,' she sighed.

It was a miniature house. She felt sure she'd seen it before. But that was weird. She'd never been up this way before. Then she realized it was one of those dream houses from inside her mind.

It had a grey roof, with four decorated chimney pots along the top. The front door had a tiny brass knocker shaped like a fancy lady in a wide hat, fixed on with screws so small you could scarcely see them. There was a letter-box that really flapped open so you could post miniature envelopes through, not that you'd need to because the door stood a little bit open, just as it should, so that children could run in and out as they wanted. There were two rows of friendly windows with real glass in them, which were urging you to peek in, past the flowery curtains. Then you'd know if the inside was just right too, if the twisty wooden stairs were there, and the happy people in the rooms, and the newly-baked cake on the kitchen table.

One thing was all wrong. The house wasn't sunny. It was in a dim corner of a dark room.

Her arms weren't holding her any more. She scrabbled and scratched to cling on but slithered backwards into the spindly plants.

'Hecking juice pigs!' She struggled to her feet. She was

31

annoyed and determined to get into the big house to look at the little house.

Luckily, some folks were stonkingly stupid about locking up. The window was open, just a crack at the bottom, quite enough to slide her skinny fingers under. With a heave, she had it up.

That dog with the teeth was here again. It smiled as she climbed in. Its side teeth looked sharp but it didn't bark. She was about to jump into the room when she was scared out of her boots to see somebody was home, right there in the room.

He was pale, lying still in a narrow bed, his head back against the pillows. Like the dog, he didn't seem to know how to make a noise. He looked like a clean dead fish. Until he rolled his eyes round and looked at her. Becks wished she'd kept that broken bit of tree. She might be going to need it.

It was no hallucination he saw, but a small child with a grubby pixie face and a large down-turned mouth missing teeth, its hair razored short all over except for a thin greasy plait at the back.

At first he thought it was a boy. But the rat's tail plait was tied with a scrap of coloured ribbon. Under a grubby anorak, she was wearing a grubby T-shirt. She had dirty fingernails, looked dangerous and was emanating so much evil.

7 Intruders and Other Villains

The child who he dimly made out squatting on his windowsill looked like one of those people from the estate on the other side of town. It was an area of such deprivation that even the patrol cars went around in threes, or so he'd heard from Mrs Murphy who had the misfortune to live there.

Was she going to mug him or menace him for money?

If so, there was absolutely nothing he could do to save himself.

His mother had recently raised precisely this scenario with Patrick and his father. What if, she had anxiously suggested, when Patrick was alone in the house, someone were to enter? What would Patrick do?

'What sort of a someone?' Patrick's father had asked with a quizzical smile.

'You know, an unwanted intruder. A drug-crazed thief,' Patrick's mother said, half smiling. And indeed it sounded so unlikely an occurrence in a quiet street like The Avenues that Patrick's father laughed.

Patrick's mother explained how she intended to install an alarm system, with a panic button within reach of the bed which Patrick would press.

The cost of this proposed installation was high. As Patrick tried to point out to her, you could build a whole primary school in Zimbabwe for that.

'But we aren't *in* Zimbabwe,' said Patrick's mother, irritably. 'And besides, you're worth more to us than the honour of having a mud-hut in Africa named after us.'

Patrick had said, 'Well, OK. So it's your house. If that's what you want to do.'

'No, darling, your house too,' his mother interrupted.

'But your money,' said Patrick. 'And Dad's. But in my

33

opinion I'm better off without it. And I've always got Attila the Hound to protect me.' Just the sound of a panic button made him feel nervous. 'And anyway, I'll be up and about in a month or so.'

Now, as he watched the wild child scrambling in over the dining-room windowsill, he wondered if his adamant rejection of a security system had been so wise.

Although he could only see one small child, there were probably half a dozen more of them out there in the shrubbery. They went around in packs, so he'd heard. He'd end up beaten to a pulp which would cause his poor old parents even more distress.

She said something. Patrick didn't understand what.

The most unfortunate loss of Miss Amy Winters' purse obliged her, all against her inclination, to recall the very first time she had been aware of being victim of theft. It was back in that sunny childhood. The theft had, curiously, been in connection with Number Seven, the doll's house which was so much in her thoughts at present. She must have been aged at least seven, for that was her age when she received the house. Possibly, she was already eight years old at the time.

Another small girl, the daughter of a colonel in the Indian Army, for those were the type of people with whom her parents associated, arrived to spend the afternoon.

Miss Winters was surprised to find that the thief's name came quite freshly to her mind: Alice.

The young visitor, on being shown into the Nursery, had run directly over to Number Seven, her mouth wide with delight and envy. 'Oh, oh, oh,' she had gasped.

'I think she likes my doll's house,' Miss Winters, or rather, Miss Amy as she then was, had observed to the young guest's nursemaid. She always wanted others to enjoy it as much as she did. 'It's called Number Seven. The houses next to it on either side would be numbered five and nine if you could see them, but of course you can't because they're only imaginary. I think seven is the best number in the world.'

Miss Alice's nursemaid had not replied for she was too busy admonishing her charge and telling her that, when out visiting, one had to greet one's hostess before descending upon their playthings.

'So say "How de do" nicely to Miss Amy, that's the way,' said Miss Alice's nursemaid. 'And keep your mouth closed or we'll all think you're out catching flies.'

Miss Alice complied.

Then the two nursemaids settled at the nursery table to gossip while Miss Amy and Miss Alice played over in the bay window with Number Seven. There was a particular inhabitant, one of the originals which had arrived at the same time as the house and its furnishings, who was most especially loved.

The Old Lady had crinkled grey darning-wool hair sewn to her head in a bun, a roundly padded body, and a constantly benign, if distant, smile painted upon her soft silk face. She wore tiny wire-rimmed spectacles attached firmly to each side of her head with three pink thread stitches.

'How do they get them so tiny?' Miss Amy had asked her nursemaid, who explained that they were not real spectacles, but the metal eye of a hook-and-eye corset fastener.

As firmly attached by stitching to her comfortable body as the spectacles were to her head, the Old Lady wore a gathered tartan skirt reaching down to her narrow, bendable, cotton-covered wire ankles. Equally irremovable were her lace petticoats, bloomers, and neat black metal boots which were also her feet. Her only item of removable clothing was a fringed plaid shawl and a straw bonnet with cotton flowers round the brim.

Since both Miss Amy's grandmothers were long since dead, the Old Lady was also known as Grandmother. Then, wearing her tiny plaid shawl, she would be seated upon the rocking chair in the parlour. At other times, the shawl was replaced by a white apron cut from a small unimportant corner of the bolster-cover on Miss Amy's own bed which nobody would ever miss, and a paper cap upon her head, marked with a red crayon cross. On such occasions, the Old Lady became a hospital matron and Number Seven was entirely given over to nursing the sick.

On the afternoon of Miss Alice's visit, when Miss Alice departed, so did the Old Lady. Amy did not actually witness Alice removing the doll. But she knew that she had.

The following day, Amy's nursemaid also noted the absence of the Old Lady. In idle moments, she played with the house just like a child although she called it, 'tidying the toys' and lingered over the task more than any other. Amy knew how she was putting part of herself inside the house.

'Miss Amy, one of your dolls is missing. The Old Lady. Have you seen her?'

Amy could not bring herself to reveal what she knew. She shook her head, thus adding falsehood to the sin of theft.

'Well, we better try to find her before your father comes up. We wouldn't want him to think we weren't taking good care of his lovely present, would we?'

Amy joined, half-heartedly, in the search, but to no avail.

When it was the day for Amy and her nursemaid to pay the return visit to Alice's home, Amy searched most thoroughly, yet discreetly. Sure enough, she quickly discovered the Old Lady secreted beneath the folded night-gown on Alice's bed. Surreptitiously she gathered her up and slipped her back into the pocket of her pinafore.

Alice had no doll's house. She had instead, a wooden Noah's Ark with the carved animals all in their pairs, and a set of skittles. Reliving the pleasure of that game of skittles, played across the wide expanse of nursery carpet while the two nursemaids sat either side of the dancing coal fire, mercifully expunged the less pleasant memory of today's theft.

What joy it was in those far-off days of childhood to be provided with a regulated space in each day for the rewards of play.

The dead fish on the bed stared with round unblinking eyes.

''Scuse us,' Becks said. 'Thought you was all out for the day.'

The dog toddled over. You never could be sure with dogs. It might be going to tear into her flesh. But no, it wanted to nuzzle its wet lips against her leg.

'Heck! Some guard dog you got yourself there,' she said. 'Flipping useless. You ought to get yourself a decent one, proper size. With attitude.'

The boy blinked but said nothing. He didn't half look scared to death.

'Rottweiler,' Becks said, as though she knew. She was glad to find she hadn't been savaged to death. 'Or a couple of Dobermanns. Just to protect you like. Anyone could get in and do you over. You need a good dog, specially in a place like this.'

She went to the house. Close to, you could see that it wasn't really made of bricks and stuff. It was all made of wood, painted, dead cunning, to look like what it wasn't. But it was old and bashed up. The paintwork was chipped to bits. One of the chimney stacks was only balanced on the roof-top. Some of the little window frames were smashed in. Some of the glass was cracked. The little front door had got teeth marks as though something had chewed it. Round Block 4 way you got bootmarks on your door when someone kicked it. Same difference.

Worst of all, slap into the middle of the front door was a big number. A metal seven, the wrong size. It was a normal number plate like you'd get on a real-sized door.

'If that was my house,' Becks said, 'I'd take care of it. Get that faffing great seven off for starters. Get one the right size. And I'd fix the chimneys. I'd see to the windows so they look nice and you could have them open. Some people just don't deserve what they got.'

She knelt down and peered in. You couldn't see a lot. It was that dark. Fancy putting the house in such a shady corner.

'It's a crying shame, you letting a place like this go to ruin.'

37

That's what Sharon used to say to the man from the Council when he came about the repairs that never got done.

Most of the rooms seemed to be empty, like a place where everybody's moved out. But then, through an upstairs window, she saw a great muddle of figures. Some were humans. Some were animals.

It would be really mivvy to live with your pet animals like that, right indoors. Except that for these people, and their pet duck and their dog, and a line of Asian women who seemed to be with them, it wasn't so ace because they were all jumbled up with their furniture on top of them. There was an old-fashioned four-poster bed like they'd got in the City Museum they could have been lying on, but it had a pink lavatory pan on it.

On the side of the house was a brass hook for opening up the front. But as she went to undo it, the boy behind her on the bed croaked, 'You're not to touch.'

'What's that? So you got a voice after all? Just going to take a quick squint. See, it's like a house I once had before, that belonged to me. Well, not really had. I saw it.' She didn't know how to say that it was not a real house she'd seen, but a house seen inside her mind. 'Just gonna find out if it's the same as what I saw. So you just lie there nice and peaceful and I won't be bothering you.'

He said, 'Take anything you want, whatever it is you're after, but I beg of you, don't fiddle with the house.'

She was peeved. 'Listen, pal, I'm not here to give you grief. I'm not one of them senseless vandals you see on the telly.'

The boy looked at her, cranky and scared. There was something about him, lying there not moving, that gave Becks an odd feeling. Not of power, more of feeling sorry for him. He wasn't like Darren or Rusna, like he could do anything to you. He was more of a helpless heap that wasn't even worth getting one over on.

'So what's up with you, matey?' she sneered. 'You a hophead or just plain pathetic?'

Then, she heard a car outside. It was stopping. A door

was being opened, then slammed. And a woman called out.

'Patrick, dear. Only me. I'm back.'

'Name's Patrick? That's pretty.'

'Go now,' said the boy. 'Please. It's better if you do.'

She looked at the little house. She didn't want to leave it. That ought to be hers. She needed it more than a boy lying in bed. She'd take care of it.

Quick as a cockroach, she made a grab for one of the tiny people shoved into the upstairs room. A little old lady, like old Ma McEwans.

He didn't notice, lying there, flat on his back like a fishy corpse.

She slid the doll into her anorak pocket. She'd keep it for a hostage. That's what you did when you wanted something off of someone else. That's what some men had done at the betting shop one time when they wanted money. They took the lollipop lady hostage. After, she got her picture in *The Courier*. Everybody saw it.

She hesitated. 'You know what, it's that gloopy, this room. You ought to do something about it. You could get someone to light you a nice little fire, like in the olden days. That'd cheer the place up for you. We seen it in the museum. You get twigs and paper and stuff. And coal. You get a maid to carry it up in a bucket.'

The boy said, 'You must go.'

'Right on. I'm off.' She scrambled on to the windowsill. 'Be back tomorrow then, old pal. Sure as houses is houses.'

8 Hot Burger, No Sweeties

The clouds shuffled themselves together into a sky traffic jam and began flinging great gobbets of rain down her neck on purpose to annoy her.

Becks was bushed. This was changing into a wet dog-sick day. She'd had enough. She wanted home. Too early. She wanted to snuggle by the secretary's hot radiator with a fluffy toffee from the lollipop lady's pocket. But you couldn't turn up without a sick note. And Sharon would never write one. She couldn't even go back and mess around in the lifts. Someone would split on her, or harass her, or try to sell her something. Sharon was right. They were all scum.

With bunking off, the day was too long. She wondered how the others got through it.

During the afternoon, despite the uncertainty of the weather, Miss Amy Winters returned to the residents' park just in case, by some extraordinary stroke of good fortune, her purse was still where she had last had it, just in case her suspicions were an entirely ill-founded work of imagination.

She walked slowly past the pond to the bench where, earlier, she had rested in sunlight. Now, it was in shadow. The wildfowl were stamping about on the grass, creating a mess of earth and soft droppings. Uneaten bread floated on the surface of the water like the swollen corpses she had seen on the River Tigris. How elusive was a mood of joy. How quickly it passed by. That was why you had to catch hold of and enjoy any such moment you could. For, whatever they said to the contrary, a time of joy was not a beauty for ever.

As she had no bag of crusts with her, the wildfowl ignored her.

Hadn't there, long ago, been a duck at Number Seven? A

tern, delicately carved from some tropical wood? But she had never much cared for it. It had such an unpleasantly smug expression. So she had placed it upon a tiny metal dish in the kitchen, as though waiting to be roasted by the maid for dinner.

It was ousted from this honourable position by the receipt, on her ninth birthday, of a set of dishes, each holding different painted plaster food, a mixed grill breakfast, a selection of colourful fancy cakes, a platter of fresh fruit, a Dundee cake spotted with dark raisins, its top patterned with almonds, and a silver-painted plaster cake-knife moulded to its side, and finally a golden-brown roast chicken surrounded by vivid emerald peas and a smear of varnish for gravy.

How eminently edible that chicken had seemed to a nine year old. The carved duck was banished upstairs to become a bathtime toy for the six rubber toddlers who tumbled, naked except for their painted red shoes, out of six Christmas crackers.

But where had that smug-beaked duck come from? All the way home, it nagged at her mind.

Of course! Miss Alice. As a makepeace gift. It had been one of the creatures from her Ark. Alice had given away one half of a duck couple.

How strange that one should still have in one's possession, well, very nearly in one's possession, for the Chambers boy was surely taking good care of the contents of Number Seven, an inanimate childhood plaything yet retain no contact with its human owner.

Miss Amy Winters wondered, what *had* become of Alice?

At last, she found the Mall. She hung around outside McDonald's till she struck lucky. She watched a woman with loads of shopping buy herself a Big Mac with fries. As she looked for somewhere to sit, she was holding her Big Mac in one hand, the carton of hot fries in the other and all her bags full of shopping flapping off her wrists. She was confused and she was in everybody's way. She placed her burger on a table and turned to untangle the shopping. Becks was in and out and away with the burger hot in her pocket as quick as a fried egg. Pity about the chips.

Then she went and hung about by the Pick 'n' Mix Sweetie Stall. While time was moving too slowly, nowhere to go and nothing to do, that house kept coming back into her head. It had two steps up to the front door. She could see it as clearly as though it already belonged to her.

A cleaner in white was sweeping up fallen sweeties. Becks darted forward to save two pink peppermint chews and a green wine gum. But the long-handled broom got there first.

'Put it down,' the sweeper grunted. 'Ain't you got no sense? That's dirty, all off the ground like that.'

Of course it wasn't dirty. The floor of the Mall was as white and shiny as the floors of heaven.

In the house with the seven on front that was too big, Becks had seen a broom like his, with real bristles and a wooden handle, though the handle was only as long as her little finger and the bristles no thicker than on a toothbrush. When the maid in the house used the broom, she never thumped it angrily like the man in the Mall.

When Becks got back, the lift was broken.

'As usual,' she said, giving the jammed doors a thump.

She had to walk up all the stinky floors to Level 5. The stairwell smelled of dogs and men.

She gave the door of flat 43 a kick to let Sharon know she was out on the landing, waiting to be let in. There used to be a door buzzer but it got broken last winter by the carol singers.

Sharon opened up and she was going ape with rage.

'And just where the fizzing heck have you been?' she screamed. She dragged Becks in by the arm. 'Look at the time, will you.' She pointed to the telly with the hand that wasn't holding Becks' arm like a pair of pliers. It was already *EastEnders*.

'And just what will the neighbours think if they know I been letting you stay out like this?'

Why should Becks care what the neighbours thought?

'You got no sense? So don't you never, never do that again, you understand?'

Before Becks had time to answer, Sharon gave her a hard slap round the head. Becks whimpered, not because it hurt but because it was simpler that way. If she ducked out of reach, Sharon would try again and it might be harder.

Becks would have to hit back. She didn't want that because they'd only end up in a big fight. And in a real fight, she knew she'd win. Then Sharon would be angry. So she'd find some other sneaky way to get back at her.

It wasn't worth the bother. Becks would play it cool. Better to lose your civil liberties but keep your mental freedom.

'And you missed your tea. So if you think you're getting money for chips off me, you're much mistaken, my girl. Go to bed with you. Now. I don't want to hear another word out of you.'

Becks went to her room as meek as a duck. She didn't mind, not the hungry gap where her tea ought to be, not the clinging cold of an unheated room, not the stinging of a slapped ear, not even the mouldy smell of the black bit of wall next to the bed where the council men wouldn't come and mend the leaky drains outside. She didn't mind any of it because inside her head she had a new place to go and in her hand she had someone to be with her.

The doll's house doll was an old lady with old-fashioned clothes and wire-rimmed glasses, though the poor thing hadn't got any ears. Underneath the crinkly grey hair, Becks saw that the glasses were sewn on to her head with pink stitches. The Old Lady didn't seem to mind. She had a calm face with a gentle painted smile.

Becks folded her fingers tightly round the Old Lady, closed her eyes and went straight up the twisty stairs to the nursery where six friendly toddlers with red shoes welcomed her in. From downstairs came the smell of a freshly baked fruit-cake just out of the oven.

* * *

How curious, reflected Miss Amy Winters as she gave Marmalade his late-night snack, that it should be, not the career successes and accomplishments of adult life, but the simple memories of early childhood which returned to be savoured in old age.

She wondered if this was true for all old people. If so, it would seem to be an essential part of a wise society to ensure that the young were given childhoods of serenity, security, and joy since it would be this early part of their existence that they would be living twice over.

However, it was far too late for her to go on fighting for children's rights. Oh yes, she had marched and speechified and protested in her time. Perhaps even accomplished a few minor changes, mostly overseas, mostly in campaigns for the basic rights of water, shelter, food. Play, paper, books came much later.

All that was done with now. She'd had her time. It was the new people's world. The young generation must resolve it the way they wanted it.

He'd supposed that Miss Winters was dumping the house on him because she hadn't room for it herself.

'Why no, my dear,' she'd said, quite agreeably. 'Quite the contrary. It is very precious to me. And is intended as an occupational therapy for you. To prevent that keen young mind stagnating and dwelling on the wretched failings of the body. For an idle brain is the devil's workshop.'

After she'd gone, his mother said, 'Astonishing old bird, must be eighty if she's a day and still so active. She's led a very interesting life, you know.'

'Yes, mother,' Patrick said. It was always simpler to agree immediately than to get dragged down into some complex parental discussion about whether old people were more deserving of concern than young ones.

He wondered if Miss Winters' spine ached as his now did, if her head went fuzzy at unexpected intervals. But so who cared if she was in agony? He certainly didn't. She'd *had* her *had* her life. She'd done things. He'd not yet begun. He might not even get *any* life.

The weeping always began so quickly. But he never let his mother see. He wanted her to think he was hard.

PART TWO
It's Wednesday

9 The Lost Lady

Patrick woke with a start, his heart pounding, as though disturbed by an unwelcome sound. Yet the house was silent. Even Attila the Hound was sleeping. Perhaps it was the unusual darkness which disturbed him?

It should not be so dark. The hall light was supposed to be left on to keep him company down here on the ground floor. Perhaps it had been turned off by an absent-minded parent. Or else the bulb had blown.

He groped for the switch by the bed. His wrists ached. He got the light on.

Something was terribly wrong, though whatever it was had already happened.

Laboriously he crossed the room to Miss Winters' doll's house, lifted the brass catch and opened up the front. In the dim light it looked so desolate in there, all those people with their possessions, their livestock, their miniature dishes of everlasting food, all bundled up higgledy-piggledy into the attic. The unhappy muddle reminded him of a stark picture in a school history book of a French château family piling their gilt chandeliers on to a hand-wagon to join the line of peasant refugees fleeing the occupying army.

He wondered if it was callous to compare inanimate figurines with real refugees in danger of their lives. Or were those black and white images of frightened people taken more than half a century ago now no more real than the inhabitants of the doll's house?

Perhaps it was just as callous to have shoved all Miss Winters' little knick-knacks into a small space where they might easily get broken. If only he'd get on and finish the repairs he could return her house and the worry would be over.

Some days, just looking at it made his body weak and his

brain blurry. The work was perfectly straightforward. Nothing he hadn't done already in first year CDT. There was fixing the banisters, a fiddly job when each was no thicker than a matchstick but not difficult, and sanding down the places where it'd been gnawed, so Miss Winters claimed, by rats when stored in an outhouse while she was abroad. There was repapering and repainting and varnishing and filling-in. And he wasn't well enough yet for any more of it.

He'd have to admit it to her, that he'd failed and she must take it back, less than half done.

He was re-closing the front when he sensed an almost imperceptible movement from within which made him shiver.

You knew they couldn't possibly be alive in there, but sometimes you felt they were looking out at you, especially the really ancient ones with the glinting glass bead eyes.

You felt that they were observing and recording all that they saw, impassive but not unfeeling witnesses to the passing of events. The toys in the house were like a Greek chorus who could watch and record but never intervene in the awesome tragedies enacted in the amphitheatre before them.

As he crouched by the house, an item of furniture toppled forward, a little Windsor-back chair which must have become dislodged when he'd opened the front.

As he carefully replaced it, he sensed rather than saw that not all the residents were home. One of them was missing.

They were a peculiar bunch: six infants made of rubber, identical except that two had lost their arms, an assortment of animals, a stern-faced Innuit-looking woman made of wood, an Edwardian maid in apron and frilly cap, a dozen papier mâché Indian musicians, a flamboyantly dressed middle-aged male in striped suit with waistcoat and gold watch, an old woman.

He woke again confused and depressed. The BBC World Service muttered on the chair beside him in a state of global timelessness. He thought of the burglar girl who'd got in. She'd said she'd be back. He wondered if she meant it. But there was nothing he could do about it.

He tossed uneasily till dawn, filled with a mixture of fear and anticipation of something awful that was going to happen.

10 Salt and Vinegar Crisps

Becks was up chirpy as a clockwork sparrow. Another yes-day for a bunk off. The lookout was ace. Somewhere to go, something wicked to do. A project, just like Mrs Whitton was always saying they had to have. Sorting out that seven on the door. The houses of the mind didn't have numbers, didn't need them.

She shoved Old Lady with no ears under the mattress. She didn't want Sharon finding her and asking nosy questions. Not that the old cow went in for bed-making, not her own nor Becks'.

'It's your bed you've made so you've got to lie on it,' she used to say.

Becks tugged the blanket over and tucked it tightly in. As she tied her trainers she thought she heard a noise like a little whimper from under the mattress. But that was naff. Old Lady was cotton wool with bendy wire legs. She wouldn't mind being squashed. It was the bed that was doing the squeaking.

Sharon was slurping sugary tea as she leaned against the kitchen sink. Her eyes were puffy. But even half-asleep, she still managed to be suspicious and narky.

'So what's got into our madam this morning? It's not even twenty to.'

'School outing. Told you last week. They taking us to one of them city farms. Got to look at cows' muck for our education.'

'You done that last term.'

'Gonna do it again, aren't we? And we got to bring fifty pee for the transport. Another fifty for the entrance.'

If she had a quid or so, Becks reckoned she could find a bus across town. That'd save time.

'Money, money. That school think I'm made of it?'

'Told you last week. Brought you back the letter about it.'

Becks lied so much to Sharon that sometimes she even began to believe the tales herself.

'Bet you never even read it. If you don't let me go, you'll have to write me a note to say so.'

Becks knew it was less effort for Sharon to give her money than find a pen and paper. Sharon wasn't much better at the reading and the writing than Becks.

Reluctantly, Sharon handed Becks a coin from the jam-jar on the shelf. 'Don't forget your dinner then.' She fetched two packets of salt and vinegar crisps out of the cupboard, hesitated, then added another. Barbecue Beef flavour.

'If it's an outing you're on, you better take three.'

'Thanks,' said Becks. Sometimes Sharon wasn't all bad.

Sharon grunted and headed back to bed.

Becks left.

The lift still wasn't mended. She skipped merrily down five flights of concrete steps.

Although this was not the day for drawing her pension, Miss Amy Winters, directly after giving Marmalade his breakfast, set out to walk to her local post office. She knew that she must report, without delay, her stolen pension book, and apply to replace it, a process which could take some weeks.

Escape from Wellend turned out to be difficult today. Everybody was on the watch-out. Could people tell, just by looking at your face, when you were doing a bunk-off?

She'd only got as far as the betting shop when, out of the All-Nite All-Rite Newsagent & General Stores, stepped Nasreen with her mum. They were always together. Some mum that. Couldn't imagine Sharon getting dressed in time to walk Becks to school.

And here they were steaming towards her. Mrs Ahmed's bold, shiny trousers flapped cheerfully in the breeze. Nasreen's tunic top and trousers were more demure.

'Hi,' said Nasreen.

'Hiya,' said Becks, slowing up to smile back, but not to stop. 'Hi, Mrs Ahmed.'

'Good morning, my dear,' said Mrs Ahmed who always spoke so politely, which was more than could be said of most of the people round here. Nothing but rubbish, that's what Sharon said. A rubbish place for refuse people. Except for the Ahmeds, probably the only honest hard-working people on the whole estate.

'Hey, Becks! You're going the wrong way!' said Nasreen laughing. 'School's *that* way!'

'Yeah, I know.'

'Where you going then?'

'Why yes, my dear, so tell us what is this terrific rush all about?' said Mrs Ahmed.

'Gotta go back, see,' said Becks.

'Back?' said Nasreen.

'Home.'

'What for?'

'Forgot my money, didn't I?'

'What money?'

'Money Miss said we had to bring in. For the collection, you know, that fund.'

'And what collection is this?' busybody Mrs Ahmed wanted to know. 'I have heard nothing.'

'You know, Nasreen. That fund Miss told us about. Them poor people in some place where they got trouble. Never mind. Better scoot or I'll be late.'

Nasreen said, 'Hey, Becks, you didn't come yesterday.'

'I was taken poorly,' said Becks.

'You should've come. Miss told us about the Country Week. At half-term. If you don't get your name down, you can't get chosen, then you can't go. You better ask her today.'

'OK. Will do.'

'And you, Nasreen,' said Mrs Ahmed sternly, 'must ask about the Special Fund.'

So Nasreen and Mrs Ahmed hurried hopefully towards Wellend Estate Primary and Becks hurried eagerly away.

When Nasreen was quietly sitting in class, patiently holding up her hand after Registration, politely asking Mrs Whitton, when Mrs Whitton finally noticed her for Nasreen rarely caused any commotion, about the Special Fund, it was a shame that the poor little Goodylocks was going to look a twit, asking after a fund that didn't exist. But that was just Nasreen's tough titty. Becks wouldn't be in range to take the rap.

She was a sound enough kid. Becks didn't want to give her grief. But just because Nasreen chose Becks as her special friend to go and see the lights last Christmas, and just because they sat next to each other, it was like the two of them were from different worlds. In Nasreen's world, you got a doting dad and mum, yellow and black jelly babies most every day, a big brother, plus so many aunties you could hardly count them, all taking care of you. In Becks' way of the world, you got nothing, except a place in the special Reading Unit on Wednesdays and a slag called Sharon you had to live with because she was your mother, both of which you could well do without.

Sharon sometimes said you had to be sorry for the poor Pakistanis, what with the way they were treated, but you could hardly feel sorry for Nasreen. She was always going to be just fine. Even the person she was going to marry, her second cousin, rich and handsome, in the sixth form at some technical college way off down in Southall, had already been sorted out for her. All Nasreen had to do was obediently go on growing up.

Becks had worries enough of her own without fretting over Nasreen. Just getting off Wellend for a start. And there was more trouble right in front of her, for through the entrance to the All-Nite All-Rite Stores Becks could see Mr Ahmed, Nasreen's uncle, selling a newspaper to Mr Fitches who used to run the betting shop. Both of them looked up. Both had nosy minds. Next, just across the road, there were Craig and Warren chucking empty drink cans at the lorries. Once they got a sniff of Becks doing a bunk, they'd want to come too. That'd ruin it.

Becks mustn't bump into anybody else who knew her. She pulled up her anorak hood to cover her face and slipped straight down the alleyway without looking back.

Miss Amy Winters hated to hear herself using that word, 'stolen', especially in connection with a small, innocent-looking child in a blue jacket, with a little pig-tail. No, she would much prefer to say, 'mislaid', or 'gone astray'. For, just supposing it had not been that child? Then these unpleasant accusing thoughts would be slander. And was not slander as bad as theft, to think ill of someone as bad as to do ill?

Becks steamed down the path to the allotments. She wasn't going to go hungry like yesterday. She'd check out more dinner in the old jacket. It better not be pickle either. All brown. Reminds you of things. And a screwdriver. Bound to be one of those in the shed. To get the seven off the door. And maybe nails. Then she'd fix the chimneys good and firm on the roof.

When she reached the shed she saw a mighty motorbike chain across the door. And a shiny new padlock. Firm as the Bank of England. Being kept out of somewhere you wanted to be in made you feel real narky. She was always on the wrong side of doors. She gave the chain an angry shake. Mean old geezer. Just when she thought she was well sorted.

'Hope he chokes on his pickle,' she muttered and set off to Town with her pound and her three packets of crisps.

11 Peppermint Cream Chocolate

Miss Amy Winters decided that, even if it *had* been that little child who had been aimlessly destroying flowers in the park, she would never, ever stand up to bear witness against her. Children should not be accused, found guilty and punished, even in areas where the magistrate leaned towards leniency. They should, rather, be given useful and constructive alternatives to petty crime which would prevent them erring again.

This was what she had done with the more wayward young folk when she was setting up the first of those centres underneath the baobab trees. Plenty of thieving there. Stupid things like broken pencil stubs and tattered reading books in a language the children did not know. Some of them had so very little, not even parents, that they'd take anything.

'Aha, Miss Winters, good to see you,' said the post office clerk, beaming through his glass screen. 'And I can guess what *you've* come about!'

He reached on to a shelf beneath his counter, straightened up and slid her purse across beneath the glass.

'Why! Goodness! How perfectly extraordinary!' Miss Amy Winters' heart missed a beat with surprise and relief. 'Wherever—?'

'A youngster handed it in yesterday. Apparently found it on the pavement just out there, said she was worried the owner might be looking for it.'

'A youngster?'

'Wasn't me spoke to her. It was the wife. Of course, she thanked her, complimented her on her honesty. There aren't many kids would take the trouble, are there? The wife gave her a bar of chocolate for her trouble.'

Miss Amy Winters opened the purse and checked its contents. Bus pass, yes. Pension book, yes. Picture of

Marmalade, yes. The one pound and sixty pence? No.

'All present and correct, Miss Winters?'

'Yes, I do believe everything's here.'

'That's a relief then, isn't it?'

'Except of course for the change.'

'Change?'

Miss Amy Winters hesitated before saying, 'Well, as a matter of fact, there was a small amount of money. Never mind. I hardly expected to see it again. And I am more than grateful to have the other items returned. Thank you so much for your part in it. I shall call by later to reimburse your wife for the chocolate.'

'You needn't bother, Miss Winters. It was nothing too much, just one of them little peppermint creams. Though if you was to insist, then it's thirty-eight pence you'll be owing.'

'Very well. Your wife didn't get the child's name by any chance, did she?'

'So's you can thank her yourself?' said the clerk, beaming. He seemed to have no idea that the purse and its contents might have been removed from Miss Winters without her consent. 'Afraid not, Miss Winters. Kiddy was in and out of here like a flash of goodness. Said she'd promised to go collecting for charity, a special fund for poor children.'

'Ah well. So she took the money but returned the other things. Let's pray she spends it wisely.'

The clerk leaned forward to speak quietly with his lips up against the screen. 'Miss Winters, that money, you are *quite* sure about it being in your purse when you mislaid it?'

'Perfectly sure,' said Miss Amy Winters. 'I recall quite distinctly counting it out before I left home to check that there would be sufficient to buy both my newspaper and some of those new vegetarian cat nuggets.' But it was pointless explaining this to the clerk. She could guess, by his patronizing manner, his private thoughts on the matter. He had absolutely no suspicion that the purse might have been purposely stolen by the child who handed it in. Rather he was of the opinion that Miss Amy Winters was another of those dotty old dears who totter down the road, spend their pension, drop their purses, forget there was nothing in them anyway, and then blame innocent citizens who are doing their best to provide care in the community.

Miss Amy Winters sensed it would be wise to desist from any further mentions of purses, pennies, and purloinings lest the clerk give her funny looks next time she came in to buy an airmail letter-form to write to her friends still working at the children's centre beneath the baobab tree.

Getting back to the boy's place wasn't as easy as your 1, 2, 3. She didn't know the surname, the house number, the name of his stupid street with the trees.

All she knew was that the little house inside his house that was like the house inside her head had a number seven on it that was the wrong size. But at least she now had a screwdriver and a saw tucked inside her anorak, and a bundle of fine big nails in her pocket as long as her hand from finger tip to wrist, and a sort of hammer thing but she didn't know what that was for.

People working on building sites hadn't a clue how to take care of their kit.

Miss Amy Winters returned to Marmalade feeling considerably more downhearted, even though she now had more of her belongings back in her possession than when she'd set out for the post office.

Theft, even a small theft, was a sad business. People had only rarely deliberately taken from her but whenever they had, it always left a pervading unpleasantness which lingered on the breath like spring onions. This unease went far beyond the loss of mere tangible items. It eroded a bit more of one's optimism in the essential benignity of humankind.

It had been one of those nights which took all day to get over. Dreams and nightmares. Sweats and pain. And a quality of repose that, however late you slept in, you still beached into wakefulness feeling completely wasted. There was stamina for nothing.

Whatever his mother optimistically said to encourage him, he knew that he was still going downhill and there was nothing, *nihil, niente,* nix, worth holding on for any more.

On mornings like this he could scarcely move. He felt he could hardly breathe. It was as though his mother's double-fronted fridge-freezer had fallen forward on to his chest. His brain went fuzzy so he couldn't any more think prolonged or complex thoughts, let alone attempt the meagre serving of homework the school sent round.

He might as well be buried up to his ears in cold mud. He might as well exist no longer and give his parents a break from their secret anxiety.

At his recognition of the long-term hopelessness of the situation, tempered only by the faint hope that his parents might give some expression of grief were he to die, he began to weep quietly, without moving, glad only that his mother had already left for work and would not hear him.

There was a woman there, half in the kitchen, half leaning out of the window, across the sink, puffing away on a fag just like Sharon did. It was disgusting the way some grown-ups did that. Didn't they care about their health?

Becks hid in a bush till, at long last and about time too, she saw the woman leaving.

For safety, she took the same route as before, scrambling through the creepers, pulling herself up on to the sill, peeking round the frame.

The house was still there. So was the boy, same as yesterday, limp and pale as cod, dead-fish eyes up to the ceiling.

Becks jumped down into the room.

'Wotcha, boy!' she said. 'Yes, it's me! Your pal, large as life. Twice as charming.'

Like yesterday, he said nothing.

'Didn't like to come in earlier. But the woman's gone out now. Your mum, is it? Gone shopping in her car with her chauffeur?'

He still wouldn't say hello and she saw that he wasn't just staring. He was crying.

'Well, I can hardly credit what I see!' Becks said. 'You're blubbing, aren't you, you great chump?'

He turned his face to the dark corner.

He wasn't just a little kid, but a teenager, probably as old as Nasreen's brother, probably old enough to use a Bic on his chin, sobbing his heart out with wet tears.

'Blub a lot, do you?'

'No. Sometimes. Yes. I dunno.'

'That makes me angry,' Becks said, the way Sharon sometimes said it, cold and even so you knew you were in big trouble. 'To see a boy blubbing for no reason.' To show how angry she was, she whammed the wall with her hand, the way Sharon's man sometimes did when he got in from the *Florida* Saturday nights.

It hurt her hand so she decided not to do that again.

'Been feeling sorry for yourself, have you? I'm telling you, old pal, I seen a lot but I never seen anything like you before, lying in bed like King Muck and still not happy.'

'Please go,' he said wearily.

'Oh no, not going this time, not when I come all this way special, to see to the little house. See, it really jibs me how you've got that seven all wrong. It's got to be changed.'

'You can't.' The boy sniffed and wiped his eyes on the duvet cover. 'That's how it's always been. It has to stay that way.'

'Why?'

'It's to do with seven being mystical.'

'Whassat?'

'Sort of magical.'

'Don't give me that. Magic's make-believe.'

'I know. But none the less, the number seven has always had special properties. In mythology, religion, folklore. You must know. Seven league boots, seven wonders of the world, seven deadly sins, the seven sleepers, seven Pleiades, sevenfold gifts of heaven.'

But Becks didn't know. 'Except about them magic boots, so you could walk ever so far once you'd got them. Miss read us that story.'

'And another thing, the person the house was built for was seven years old.'

'So all this magic stuff makes it so special you don't want no one never touching? Made of invisible gold, I suppose? Looks to me like the whole thing could do with a lick of magic paint. Or else you could put a match to it.'

She gave it a prod with her trainer, not to hurt it, more to grieve him. He didn't deserve it.

He flinched. 'Please don't kick it. That's glue along the balustrade. It's meant to be setting.'

'Wasn't kicking. Just asking.'

'It's an antique. Well, sort of. It's old. Belongs to a lady from down the road. I'm repairing it for her.'

'Oh, yeah. Don't see the evidence.'

'I'm working on it. It takes skill and time.'

'Wouldn't take a jiffy to fix them chimneys. Look, I even got the nails. You need to fix them before they fall.'

'Your nails are wrong,' he said. 'They'd split the wood. You have to use panel pins.'

'Go on, then. Show us.'

'They're in the box under the bed.'

Becks looked, found and dragged out the tool-box. There was all the stuff for miniature house repairs in there, the little tools, and glues and paint pots, and the sandpaper and wallpaper and little finicky bits of wood. He'd got all this stuff together but he hadn't bothered getting on with it. He was weird.

12 Happy Families

The morning of her seventh birthday began as any other day. Her nursemaid got her up. There were lessons of Arithmetic and French with the governess at the nursery table. There was luncheon with the nursemaid, the usual colourless food, braised tongue and steamed potatoes, followed by tapioca and rhubarb, boiled till it had taken on the same grey shade as the boiled tongue and transparency as the tapioca.

Later in her life, when she had shared joyous family meals of mealie, of puri, of sadza and maizemeal ugali, with Zimbabweans, Pakistanis, Mexicans, or Ugandans, Miss Winters came to consider how dull and unimaginative were those repetitive nursery menus of her privileged childhood.

Only after the silent luncheon did the routine of her day change. Instead of walking to the park to observe the ducks, the nursemaid obliged her to have forty minutes rest on her bed with her dampened hair in curling rags. Then the nursemaid got her up again, untied the rags and brushed out the curls. She dressed her in her best frock with the wide starched collar that scratched against her neck, and it was time to go down to take tea with her mother. Miss Amy became nervous with anticipation.

The nursemaid knocked on the drawing-room door.

'Enter, O fairest princess,' boomed out Mr Winters' voice. So he was there too. How very strange.

Miss Amy went in and her nursemaid went away, for on Miss Amy's birthday, she had the rest of the afternoon off.

Amy's mother, wearing her best flowery muslin afternoon frock, was seated. Her father was standing with his back to the fire. And on a low stool between them sat the little house.

The downstairs maid carried in the tray with the silver tea-pot, the silver cream jug, the silver sugar basin and the tea-cups that made music when they rattled. But Amy noticed none of it. Her eyes were upon the house. So perfectly made, so like a real house that she felt she could walk right into it.

Becks fixed the chimneys, tapping down the panel pins like the boy said. Then she shoved the tool-box back under the bed and noticed food on the floor. It was some yellow eggy mess, with bits of burned toast round the edge.

It was funny how even horrible-looking food reminded you of feeling hungry. The only time she'd ever felt so full she ached was that time she went to eat at Nasreen's place. Nasreen got a hot meal every day of her life.

'Cor, you leaving all that lot?' she said to the boy. 'Myself, I'd kill for a nice plate of hot chips, wouldn't you?'

He peered at her over the duvet. He was that nervy.

'Only a manner of speaking, old pal. You know what I mean, you got anything else?'

He nodded. 'Yes. I mean, no. I mean, I'm not really sure. I suppose so. You'd have to go and help yourself. In the fridge.'

'Grand. Because I don't fancy picking at your manky leftovers. Along the passage, is it?'

'And across the hall.'

Becks took one of the people from the house with her when she went to find the kitchen. It was awesome. The whole of one of the flats in Block 4 would've fitted in, with space over for a jacuzzi. It was like one of those photo kitchens in Sharon's shopping catalogue which didn't look real because everything matched and all the mess had been tidied away.

The fridge was just wicked. One of those tall ones with the double doors. Big as the Wendy house in the Infants' class. You felt you could walk right into the white ice world.

Her breath made fluffy clouds in the cold air.

Becks hopped the doll out of her hand and into the fridge. This one was a maid. Becks could tell because she had a white apron, and a frilly white cap sewn on to her yellow frizzy hair like the servants' costumes they'd seen in the museum when Miss was telling them about the olden days.

The mega-fridge was lit inside by spot-lights at different levels like the big stores at Christmas time. Just packed with stuff. Cans of fizzy, yoghurts all flavours, mini-pack cheeses all colours, apricot juice, apple, pineapple, tomato, mixed fruit. Eight shelves, stacked with other stuff in bright packets. Freezer stuffed full. Ice-cream, six tubs, three flavours, pink and white strawberry shortcake and cream, brown Belgian chocolate with dark chocolate bits, green pistachio. Sorbet, frozen pizza, frozen gâteaux.

Becks stared. Too much food to be real. She was really surfing. With the Maid sitting there expectant, Becks knew she was entering a magic food store, like the *World of Food* in the Mall, except just for doll people. Becks let the Maid hop along a shelf to inspect some yellow chickens on the side of a packet of chick-burgers.

All was so pure and bright and gleaming white, not like the crummy cut-price place up the end of Grimsy Street where Sharon did her shopping, with sawdust on the floor and speedy cockroaches darting for the corners.

By staring hard, Becks could see fridge families, mums and dads, toddlers and twin sisters, in their white fur-trimmed anoraks like Eskimos, sauntering from one shelf to the next with their miniature trolleys.

The people from the doll's house were too posh to do their own shopping. That's why they sent their Maid.

Becks leaned on one of the fridge doors. As it closed, the store's illuminations dimmed. It was midnight. Soon be closing time. The miniature manager's voice came over the speakers, not like the sweetie sweeper in the Mall but polite and friendly like Nasreen's uncle, Mr Ahmed.

'Esteemed customers. Please complete your purchases and proceed to the exits. Thank you. Please come again to our world of food. Enjoy, enjoy, enjoy.'

There were no pay-desks. This was cash-free shopping.

'Better hurry,' Becks said to the Maid. She found a life-

sized china plate in one of the tidy cupboards. She let the
Maid skip round the shelves picking stuff out. What Becks
really wanted was a big bagful of sizzling hot chips, sprinkle
of salt, dash of vinegar, loads of tomato ketchup. But she'd
have to make do with this other stuff that the Maid was
picking up.

When the plate was heaped high, they carried it back to
where the bed-weirdo lay.

'The house,' said Amy's mother, 'is your gift from Papa, and
these are from me.' She pointed to the two small packets
before the house.

'What do you say to your father?'

Amy had no idea what had to be said. She felt that her
voice, her thoughts, her everything had been taken from her
by this view of the miniature house with her own number,
seven years old, gleaming on the tiny door.

'It's for you, dear,' said her mother.

One of the parcels contained the first item of furniture for
the house, a miniature four-poster bed, smaller even than a
wooden pencil case.

'And who's going to sleep in there, I wonder?' Amy's
father said.

Inside the other wrapped packet were the first inhabitants
of the house, a set of six stiff dolls with wire limbs, metal
feet, and painted satin smiles.

Miss Amy was so astonished by the house, all her own, to
live in, that she was unable to drink her tea from the tinkling
china cup, nor eat a single sliver of the walnut cake baked
specially for her birthday.

13 Cheese, Chocolate, and Squirty Cream

The robber-girl wasn't causing any trouble, just chattering away to herself. He couldn't be bothered to make her go. He let her see to the chimneys and was relieved to discover that she was careful. She had small hands and was good at it, so long as he explained carefully. Then she began to sort through the contents of the house, inspecting each piece of furniture, setting everything on the carpet, muttering to the dolls to be patient. It was restful having her there, certainly more reassuring than Attila the Hound wandering stupidly about wagging his tail.

She replaced the furniture, not as she had found it, jumbled upstairs, but sorted methodically according to use. He watched how intensely she gazed into the darkness of the house like a chess player before a move, as though considering exactly where each item would go to its best advantage.

There was a wooden towel-horse, a work of supreme Lilliputian craftsmanship, which she turned over and over in the palm of her hand trying to work out what it was for. She gave up and put it in the parlour. A towel-rail in a parlour! Like keeping coals in the bath.

He was beginning to feel better. Not really better, but certainly less anxious.

She went off somewhere and returned with one of his mother's dinner-party plates piled high with an unruly compost heap of sweet and savoury, desserts, yoghurts, cheese triangles, mini choc swiss rolls, all mixed up together. She had squirted a thick trail of aerosol cream over everything.

He watched as she settled herself cross-legged on the floor

to attack this feast. He wondered why he'd thought that she might be dangerous. She didn't look like a thief. She was more like some kind of small, semi-domesticated forest creature. As she ate, she made sub-human grunting noises. It was disgusting, yet somehow mesmerizing, to see how she shovelled food into her open mouth like a pig at the trough. When bits dropped out, she ignored them and plunged her hands back into the plateful for more.

'You got a big family here?' she asked through a full mouth.

'No.'

'Just wondered. Because you got enough food back there to open up your own night shelter. For poor people. Them ones that hang around in the Mall and get drunk.'

'I have no siblings. There's me and my parents.'

'Uhuh. So maybe it's just your mum's got one of them shopping diseases. You know, can't help buying stuff?'

She clutched an Italian breadstick to use as a kind of spoon, stirring it round in a puddle of chocolate mousse, then drawing it out to lick off the slippery slime.

After unwrapping a cheese triangle, she changed her mind, bit into a ripe black fig, then spat it out.

'Yerghk,' she said and tried a handful of dark Californian cherries.

There was all this exotic fruit his mother kept buying in to try and tempt him back to a healthy hunger. Goodness knows what it cost in aviation fuel to fly fruit round the world.

The girl paused, breathless from scoffing, and held her plate out to him.

'Sure you don't want to try a bit? It's right good.'

He thought of those starving African crowds crammed into their feeding centres that took up so much of his parents' cash and concern. He wondered if they had ever considered that some of the world's starvers might be nearer than they realized.

She was trying to eat a cream-filled chocolate profiterole. She must have taken it straight from the freezer for it was frozen solid. She had no front teeth and couldn't even get a grip on it.

Finally, she pushed the plate to one side and, after wiping her chocolate-brown fingers on the carpet, she snapped open a can of Icelandic mineral-water which she drank with a noise like the bath-water running away down the plug-hole.

'Couldn't find no Coke. This stuff's weird. Don't taste of nothing at all,' she said. She burped with satisfaction as she slurped it down.

'Well then,' she said. 'So what's up with you? Got the same problem as your house? You some kind of broken-down antique?'

'No.' Patrick hated talking about the illness to strangers. It made it seem so definite.

'But you was in bed yesterday and all. It looks like you're some kind of permanent bed-boy.'

It was bad enough having his father coming in every single morning to ask in a hushed and reverent tone, 'Slept a little better last night, I hope?' You could almost touch the anxiety in his voice. You just had to keep saying 'Yes' to reassure him.

'Really sick or putting it on a bit? You don't look regular ill, just a bit peaky. Sort of cold and sticky like a frog.'

He wanted to tell her that on the topic of frogs, she was correct that they were cold, but wrong to believe that they were sticky. Perhaps she had never seen, let alone touched, a frog. Suddenly, he couldn't stand the silly child's chatter rattling round his head. He couldn't stand anything. He knew his head pain was coming back. His legs had begun to throb again. The vision was growing fuzzy.

'Will you go? Please go now. I must get some rest,' he snapped. Then he couldn't help adding, 'Yesterday you removed one of the people.'

To his surprise, she didn't try to deny it.

Petulantly, she stuck out her chocolate-smeared lip. 'So?' she said.

'So. You now must put it back.'

'Can't. Ain't got her on me. She's back home under me blanket having a little kip because she's so old. Didn't you know that's what old folks have to do to keep them fresh?'

'Then you must return home and fetch it.'

'Can't get in. Ain't got no key and my mum's out. She does this little job lunchtimes, Wednesday and Friday. Cleaning up down the *Florida*. Anyway, it was only the one I took. You still got all them others. They're in there. I put the babies to bed. They was tired.'

'They are not mine. I told you. They belong to someone else. And the dolls must all remain with their house so they can do their job.'

'Their job? You barmy? Dolls don't have no jobs.'

'Their work is to mark the passage of time and to constantly observe, without judgement, all events which occur within their hemisphere.'

He closed his eyes.

When she had been sitting quietly she'd been no trouble. But already this short confrontation had exhausted him.

The terrible roaring rushing waterfalls of the tinnitus disturbances filled his head from ear to ear.

She looked at him with her head on one side. 'You really *are* poorly, aren't you? You poor old geezer, you.'

'And you really are completely untrustworthy.'

She said, 'If I brings the Old Lady back tomorrow, can I stay and fix them little wobbly stairs for you?'

Watching the national news with Marmalade upon her lap, Miss Amy Winters found herself strangely distanced from the events being revealed. It was as though they no longer concerned her.

'You see, Marmalade,' she said, 'the fact is, I am not as much involved in the world as once I was. And I fear that I have minimal concern for the current re-shuffle of our Cabinet.'

Marmalade purred noisily like rattling bones and flicked his tail.

'And nor, I suspect, do you. For all cats are grey in the dark.'

Miss Winters knew that those many years of living in far-away lands, with only her postal vote to connect her to the elections of the government, had already eroded much of her interest in home affairs. And, in addition, those countries where she went to work seemed always to have so many of their own tumultuous difficulties.

'So, Marmalade, my friend, are we to accept these enlightened proposals of the new Minister for Social Affairs to provide more amenities, nursery places, play-schemes, privatized policing, and trees on the urban housing estates? Indeed, do we even believe them?'

Marmalade jumped down from her lap and went off to nuzzle the door of the pantry.

'Sadly, the answer to both questions is No.'

While it was perfectly reasonable for the cat to have no political interests, Miss Winters suspected that it was a failing in herself as an intelligent human to be growing so inward-looking, to be more concerned about her own well-being, her own memories of the past, than about the world.

'But times change and we with time, eh, puss?'

When an image of 10 Downing Street filled the television screen, it was the image of Number Seven which filled Miss Winters' mind. And with that image came a stab of loss.

She did miss it so much. It was her house, her property, containing the souvenirs of her past. She had every right to want it back. She must reclaim it before that useless young lad did it any harm.

She would go round at the first possible opportunity and explain to that nice Mrs Chambers how she needed the house back. That nice Mr Chambers must drive it round in his car.

She must get it back before it was too late, for a stitch in time saves nine.

PART THREE
Seven Days Make One Week

14 Fuzzy Narkhead

Sometimes the loneliness became unendurable. His mother would be gone for hours and, though he resented her persistent cheerfulness when she was there, he missed her when she wasn't. He had to listen to the silence, and to the sounds of the house breathing, or not breathing.

He wondered if, in the end, this virus did kill you through fear and loneliness if not the effects on the body. Anyway, he wasn't much afraid of dying. It might be better if he were, to add an icy sharp edge to his existence.

Fear was bad, but isolation was always going to be worse.

Tomorrow I'm going to come and help you. That's what she'd said, hadn't she?

He felt a foolish lurch of anticipation. For a bed-slug, he was almost excited.

Few visitors came now. They'd got bored. People of his age were supposed to be out and about, full of vigour, skateboarding down the pavement frightening old ladies. Even his best mates were all wrapped up in their Trials.

'Look, pal, I've got your dolly here, see. I'm not saying anything about her. I'm just putting her back in the little house, OK? No messing. I haven't hurt her or nothing. So you don't need to worry.'

She thought he said, 'Thank you,' but if he did, it was so quiet you could hardly hear.

He was slowly covering the polished table with newspaper. Then just as slowly he was setting out his tools like it was a workshop. Then he got her to help lift the house on to the table. He said it was so it'd be easier to reach when they were working on it.

Then, suddenly, before they'd done anything, he was

tired. He asked her to go. Or rather, he told her she'd got to go.

The day after when she turned up, he was in the bed, miserable as a shivering dog. Day after, up again, in an armchair, but couldn't even tell her what to do.

'So I'll decide for myself, shall I?' she said, chirpy as a sparrow in a tree. 'You know what, on your off days, they ought to use you for a bed-warmer down the old people's home.'

She set to polishing the brass fittings on the front door, including the big seven, then the brass wind-up knob on the underneath of the clockwork piano.

'It's not a piano,' he managed to say. 'It's called a harpsichord.'

'Same difference,' she said.

And when she'd polished anything that could be polished, she opened his tins of enamel paint and touched up the painted flames in the parlour fire-place, then the yellow almonds on top of the Dundee cake on the kitchen table.

Patrick knew the thief girl was right. He *did* cry a lot. Usually nobody saw, except for Attila the Hound. But now there was always her, seeing and making judgements.

Irritably, he muttered, 'Just because a person's not one hundred per cent fit doesn't mean they have to be some bonehead macho-man all the time.'

And why shouldn't he weep when he needed to? Sometimes it even seemed to help relieve the tension.

He lay watching as she found a pair of pliers to fix the hinges of the oven door.

'The kitchen range is German-made, probably about 1920.' He started to tell her its historical provenance though she didn't seem very interested.

It stood on four clawed feet, like an Edwardian bathtub. There was a set of copper pots and pans to go with it. He watched her polish them furiously, till they were shiny as gold. Inside the range was a socket to place a wax night-light which, if lighted, heated the hot plates so they sizzled when you spat on them.

The girl was getting to do all the interesting repairs. She was getting all the satisfaction. It was miserably unjust.

Becks, coming up the driveway, saw that woman in the blue overall sitting in the kitchen. She was puffing away on a fag and had a mug in the other hand. Becks used to think she was the mother. But she wasn't.

The woman saw Becks.

'Yes?' she said, looking down at Becks as though she was a bit of dog dirt on the doorstep.

'I come to see the boy,' said Becks. 'I got him something.'

'They're nice people here. They got nice things in their home. Madam don't like me letting strangers in.'

'*I'm* let in. *I'm* his best mate. *I* been helping him.'

'Oh yes, I don't think.' The woman squinted at Becks through a cloud of cigarette smoke, then said in a surly way, 'I *know* you, don't I?'

'Expect so. I been coming here for years and years.'

'Like heck you have. You're from up our way, aren't you? I seen your mum in the *Florida*. She works there and all.'

'Maybe.'

'Whatever it is you've come about, get it over quick because I'm off as soon as I finished my cup of tea.'

The original plan was that the house would help his History Project, 'Development of vernacular house-styles through two tempestuous centuries.'

Try explaining that to a doll-thief from Wellend who couldn't even read simple instructions on the side of a tube of balsa cement for sticking a chair-leg. 'It says,' he read out, 'that it is a quick drying cement for wood and general purpose use. Transparent, waterproof, insulative. Thinly coat each surface and briefly hold until set. It also says, "Warning. Highly Flammable. Do not use near fire or naked flame".'

The warning was printed in four languages. English, French, Italian, Spanish. The French word for 'Inflammable' was the same as the English word. That might be useful to remember for when he got to taking the French exam.

In his History Project, he'd decided that it would conclude in the nineteen thirties, those years of class divide, of working-class deprivation, with the middle classes still living in comfortable, genteel ignorance with their maids and their gardeners, while the bottom-of-the-pilers had less than next to nothing.

The parents were pleased with his project though he had dismissed their approval with a disinterested shrug. His mother located a woman for him to interview. She was a receptionist at the Social Advice Bureau whose great-uncle had walked with his wife, in the quest to find work during the Depression, from Norwich to Glasgow pushing three children in a perambulator.

Patrick hadn't yet written up those interview notes. Probably, he never would. Each day there was less energy, less hope, less joy, less future. No doubt much the same as for that long-ago out-of-worker on the road to the shipyards of the Clyde. These days, Patrick wasn't even getting out to buy his own glue and sandpaper. It wasn't fair.

Becks knew she'd been right that first time she saw him. The house was the mivvy, not him. He was a crabby narkhead. But you couldn't have one without the other. They went together, like Nasreen and Mrs Ahmed.

'Before I come along, you wasn't doing nothing about it anyway, was you?' she said. 'You just had it all sat there in the dark, all for yourself. You wasn't even looking at it then, was you?'

He said, 'I've ordered some books from the library. Well, I mean my mother did. To help with getting the detail right.'

He handed her the book. 'Look, it explains here how the interior decorations should be. Pelmets, dados, that sort of thing.'

Becks looked at the page he held open. 'Just words,' she said. She flicked over to the next page. More words, and a diagram. 'I told you before. I don't read words.' She slapped the book shut.

'There's pictures too. But you ought to learn.'

'Can't.'

'Can't be bothered, more like,' said Bedboy. He reached for the book where she'd let it fall on the duvet and began to read aloud.

'If you're going to nag at me like some teacher, I might as well bog off,' Becks said.

'No. Please don't go. Stay.'

15 Heather Honey for Sweetness

Miss Amy Winters, making her cautious way down The Avenues, with a jar of heather honey for the boy and a posy of roses from the front garden for the mother, recalled young people from the past who had been felled, as the Chambers boy apparently was, by the devastation of disease from which sometimes, but not always, they recovered.

Measles, whooping cough, poliomyelitis. There had been a first cousin who contracted tuberculosis of the hip and was rendered lame and sterile. She herself had briefly enjoyed the existence of a younger brother until an epidemic of measles arrived in the neighbourhood like a bad fairy. In the days before inoculation, measles was often a child-killer. Curiously, although she too had been extremely ill, she had survived.

She recalled Mother and Father overwhelmed with grief, unwilling even to come up to the nursery. Eventually they had looked beyond their loss to see that a quiet daughter who survived had as much right to recognition and attention as a beloved son who perished.

In those far-off days, parents were in anticipation of serious illness and were less surprised, if no less distressed, when it claimed victims.

'The difference today,' said Miss Winters aloud, forgetting for a moment that Marmalade was not with her, 'is that parents in the West expect their little ones to live the full span. It's no small wonder the Chambers parents are distraught.'

So, Miss Winters, reaching the gate-posts with the lions on top, resolved to modify the nature of her call. It would be social. She would enquire after the health of the boy without, initially, mentioning her pressing need for the return of

Number Seven. Only when the moment seemed right, would she ask, as though in passing, for its speedy return.

Becks said, 'Look, I made them their telly.'

It was an empty matchbox. She stuck a bit of white paper over one side to be the screen. She scribbled some round black blobs to be the control buttons. She drew a man's head and shoulders on the patch of white paper.

'That's the news man. With the bow tie. They're watching the news.'

She put the matchbox carefully on the kitchen table. 'Pity it can't really turn on. Then they'd turn over and watch the cartoons on the other channel.'

Bedboy sat up. 'It can't go in there,' he said.

'I know. It's only in the kitchen till I think of somewhere better. It's for the Maid to watch.'

'It can't go in there at all. They don't have television.'

''Course they do. Everybody has television.'

'These people do not.'

'Why not? They some kind of hippies? Or squatters? Don't look like squatters to me, not with all that furniture they got. And the flipping maid.'

'They do not have television,' Bedboy said firmly, 'because their house, although designed in late Georgian style, is furnished in the style of the late nineteen twenties. Nineteen twenty-seven, to be precise, and nobody had television.'

'Why?'

'Because Baird had scarcely finished perfecting his invention.'

'No. I mean, why that time you just said? Why can't it be now this minute inside the house?'

'Because that's the way it is.' He lay down.

Becks shrugged and removed the matchbox. He was weird.

'OK, suit yourself,' she said. It didn't look much like a proper telly anyway.

* * *

81

The visit was briefer than Miss Winters intended. The mother was not home, nor the father, nor their cleaning woman. It was a young child who came to the door and who insisted that Miss Winters come right in and speak to the sick boy in his bed even though Miss Winters herself expressed the wish only to leave her small gifts upon the hall table and depart.

'Oh no, he ain't doing nothing, just laying there pathetic so you might as well come in and take a peek,' the child said. She was strikingly familiar. Miss Winters had met her before. Perhaps the Chamberses had taken her in as a foster child just as she herself had taken in Blessings when the mother had drowned in the river. This child seemed entirely at ease here, just as Blessings had throughout the seven years she had housed her.

The child trotted ahead leading the way down a dark passage to the room where Miss Winters immediately, and to her immense relief, saw her dear Number Seven safe and sound. The front panel was open and the little figures had been placed outside, some upon the dining chairs and armchairs, others seated upon the floor, all of them waiting expectantly.

They were, of course, waiting to be fed, just like hungry crowds the world over. The child crouched down and set before them the brightly painted plaster dishes, each one the size of a two-shilling piece. The yellow roast chicken with its surround of vibrant green peas was given to the old grandmother, raised veal pie for the nursemaid, Dundee cake for the tin dog.

The vision of a lone female rationing out meals to a large but patient crowd was strangely unsettling to Miss Winters, reminding her too closely of herself at some bleak and dusty feeding centre with the ladle and the big black pans of mealie.

She turned away to pay attention to the invalid. He looked desolate enough, flat on his back, an eiderdown to his chin, the complexion clammy. She patted his hand which was lifelessly cold and she placed the honey on the chair beside him.

'So, my dear, I'll be on my way for it's idle folk like me who have the least leisure. And I'm glad to see you're wrapping up warm, that's the main thing, for if we are to believe the wisdom of Hippocrates, one must be wary of sudden changes, though the very best doctors are Dr Quiet, Dr Diet, and Dr Merryman. Don't mind me. I'll see myself out.'

She departed hastily, feeling confused and dismayed. The child playing on the floor was the pickpocket who had stolen her purse. They say that a guilty conscience needs no accuser, yet that child's face was a pool of innocence as she created her imaginary world of serenity.

'Goodbye, Miss Winters. Thank you for coming to see me. I'll let my mother know,' the boy whispered after her. 'Thank you for the jam.'

She did not stop to correct him, to explain that it was not jam but honey, a natural product, full of healing goodness.

Oh my, but what a walk it was, from their end of The Avenues, back down to this end. Still, she mustn't give up yet for it was only the good died young.

As she made her way home, Miss Winters pondered deeply on the needs and wants of the young. It had been, in her experience, not enough just to set up feeding centres to provide the children with meals. That was but a first step which prevented them remaining listless, and susceptible to sickness.

'Well begun is but half done,' she used to tell her colleagues when they thought a job was complete. The next, and equally important step was to take care of the intake of the children's minds, to nourish the intellect, to feed them with ideas, to give them the opportunity to play creatively so that they might learn to think creatively.

Initially, this had to be done in some of the simplest ways, with wooden building bricks, and where there was no wood, with home-styled cardboard building bricks, with mosaic pattern shapes, later with crayons and paper, but above all with creating a situation for constructive play.

That had often been one of the first problems. Many of

those impoverished children quite starkly did not know how to play. When you began to teach them, the impoverished adults complained.

'So what he doin' with them wooden blocks, wasting his time, ma'am? Why he no readin' and writin'?'

Play was seen as a luxury of which few, in those harsh times, recognized the true value. Many of her schemes had been dismissed by her colleagues as mere frivolity. She had even received an official reprimand from above for misuse of funds. Not till much later was the value of her work recognized.

However, Miss Winters must remember now that, though Brag was a good dog, Holdfast was better. She had learned more from the world than she had taught the world and she must not lose sight of what she had learned. She must not allow this unfortunate possessiveness of old age to take hold. There must be a sharing of every one of the resources of the world, even down to a cherished toy house.

She had seen, with her own eyes, how the pickpocket was purposefully absorbed. She must reverse her decision to reclaim Number Seven. She must leave it where it was for the child's use.

'For as the twig is bent, so is the tree inclined,' she declared to Marmalade who was waiting right there on the mat inside the front door to welcome her home.

16 A Place of Sanctuary

His mother decided to be anxious again about strangers in the house. She said, 'Of course I'm glad you had someone to keep you company. But you must understand, Patrick, that waif ought by rights to be in school.'

'Why d'you always have to interfere in everything?'

'Unless children are in exceptional circumstances, as you are, with a medical certificate to prove it, it's a legal requirement that they attend school.'

'She hates the dump she has to go to. Anybody would. Conditions are appalling up there. You've seen it on the telly. She's bullied. There's drugs. People steal things from her. The teachers don't like her.'

'You know all that's beside the point.'

'It's better her being safe in here than wandering about the streets. Anything might happen out there.'

'There's another thing. She shouldn't be let in when you're alone. I don't like it. Nor does your father.'

'I thought you were so worried about me being on my own? Now you're worried that I'm not alone. What's all this changing sides?'

'Patrick, you don't understand. You never know what people might *think*. And you don't know what she might get up to. There's something about her I can't put my finger on.'

'She plays with Miss Winters' house, that's all. There's no harm in that.'

'It was, as a matter of fact, Miss Winters who alerted me to this problem.'

'It wasn't a problem before you made it one,' Patrick muttered. 'I wish I could live my own life without you always telling me what to do.'

'Miss Winters told me she was extremely concerned about the welfare of the little girl she saw here.'

'And what's that supposed to mean?' His mother picked up his supper tray off the floor. 'I know what you meant. That she's dirty, that she smells, that she's probably got lice. With my immune system so disadvantaged, I'll catch anything that's around. That's what you meant, isn't it?'

'Patrick, please let's not get into an argument. I just want you to know that we know the child comes in here and we'd rather she didn't.'

'You mean, she's banned? Mr and Mrs Wonderful Liberal Save-the-World are introducing their very own apartheid against Wellend scruff? And what about Mrs Murphy? Is she banned too?'

'Patrick, you're deliberately misreading me. I'm advising you to discourage the child from coming here. And as for Mrs Murphy, yes, as a matter of fact I have suggested she might be happier in a different job.'

'You've sacked her?'

'No, just reminded her about our policy on smoking indoors. I've told her that I'll try to find her another position where it wouldn't be a problem.'

Patrick marvelled at his mother's ability to stab harshly but with a gloved hand. He wondered if he could do the same to Becks.

Bedboy was talking religions. He called it Theology. Becks only half listened when he got going on one of his themes.

'I'm seeing about the little carpet next,' she said. 'The one what the butterflies ate.' You had to fill in the cross-stitch pattern wherever bits were missing with coloured threads.

'Not butterflies. Moths,' he corrected her. 'And not really moths either. It's their grubs.'

'Make up your mind.'

At least, she *thought* it was religion he'd been on about. Sometimes when he talked posh you couldn't tell. When they'd done Religion at school Mrs Ahmed came in and told Assembly about the mosque. But she was a Pakistani. It was different from what he was on about.

86

'I've been reconsidering my GCSE choices,' he said.

'Oh yeah,' she said.

'I've decided to change from Physics to Philosophy. Philosophy sounds interesting. You get to discuss abstractions. Like Personal Responsibility, Faith, the Proof or otherwise of the existence of God.'

'Round our part,' Becks said, hoping to be useful, 'most of that kind of thing's closed up now.'

He said, 'Don't talk nonsense. You can't close up God.'

Becks wondered how to tell him that the things that went on inside his head as he lay there, and what went on at Wellend, were not the same. Inside his head was pretend. Up Wellend was real. She said, 'See, it's like this. We had this church one time, but it's locked. Boards across the door. Bars and wire and stuff on the windows. Sharon says that's because God's gone over to join the Tories, left us lot to stew in our own stink.'

'You mean, out there you have no place of worship?'

'Not unless you want to go round the mosque. But you gotta be one of them to join in.'

'So for the rest of you, there's no parish priest to take care of you?'

'There's our lollipop lady. She's ever so lovely. Takes care of the little ones crossing the road. Takes care of the school. That's why they call her the Caretaker. And there's Mrs Ahmed, runs toddler group and Wednesday Special Reading.'

'I understand the social element. But who is left for your community's spiritual guidance?'

This naffhead had done so much bed-warming there was nothing left inside his brain.

Becks said, 'Dunno. Look, you'll have to thread me needle again. It's all come undone.'

Miss Winters' body was strangely tired today. Dull indistinct aches wandered across her back and joints. Although the spirit remained keen, the outer casing was definitely growing weary through use. Eventually it would be beyond repair.

'But nothing too serious so far,' she reassured Marmalade. 'Just a normal indication of the ageing process. No doubt you'll feel the same thing in your time.'

Marmalade, sprightly and still in the prime of his life, had at least another seven years of activity left in him, providing he crossed the road carefully and kept up with his feline flu jabs. Perhaps her second cousin's son in Australia would help with those. After all, she was leaving him everything she had.

Marmalade jumped with pain-free agility on to the windowsill, settling down to stare intently at passing clouds.

In view of today's temporary fatigue, Miss Winters decided she would do better to abandon the morning walk and, following Marmalade's example, take it easy.

She pushed and pulled and shoved her armchair from its usual place between the low card table and the gasfire, over towards the window.

'Instead of my constitutional,' she told Marmalade, who was keeping his back towards her as he gazed unblinking at the sky, 'I'll sit here by my window and I shall enjoy the day this way. I shall have just as much fun being a passive onlooker as an active participant.'

Gently, she lowered herself to the chair. Seated, she had a view of the rose-bush in front of the window. She observed how the delicate new stems and leaves now surging with life were not so much green as a burnished golden red. A quite surprising colour for a leaf to be, she thought to herself, though she did not make this observation aloud for the fact that roses came in such an infinite variety and subtlety of shades was not something she thought would be of interest to Marmalade.

17 Sanctions

Bedboy had given himself a nasty headache with too much thinking. So she'd fetched a tea-towel from the bright clean kitchen, wetted it under the cold tap, folded it into a tidy rectangle and put it on his face. She told him to lie quiet while she got on just like the school secretary did that time when Sharon made her go into school even though she'd already caught the Chinese flu.

Bedboy lay so still it was like he'd stopped breathing. Peaceful. Becks got on with the work that had to be done, scraps of wallpaper, nail-scissors, glue brush, and all the household sitting outside looking on while she repapered their parlour walls, except for Wooden Woman. Her legs were rigid so she always had to stand. Becks didn't speak aloud to any of them. There was no need. They could hear what was in her mind.

She explained how fiddly the job was, how it had to be done carefully, how good their parlour was going to look when the decorating was finished, and how she liked doing it for them.

In return she felt the warmth of their approval. Even Wooden Woman's flat gaze as she leaned stiffly against the wall seemed to be full of friendliness and gratitude.

Bedboy ruined it all by speaking. He was a great one for talking.

'Rebecca?' he said from under the wet cloth.

'Right here, Flowerpot.' The school secretary had called her that when she'd fainted in class with the Chinese flu.

'I've been thinking.'

'Uhuh.' Nothing new there. He did a lot of that.

He took off the cloth and she could see those pale watery eyes.

'If you want this arrangement to carry on, I'm going to

have to make demands of you. It's become apparent that my moral duty is to put you on the right path.'

'Oh yeah.'

'There's going to have to be the imposition of some sanctions.'

'So what's a stonky sanction when it's at home?'

'It means you will have to abide by one basic rule.'

Becks pasted the back of the patterned paper strip that was to go round the walls of the parlour. A decorative floral frieze, Bedboy called it.

He said, 'You do like coming here?'

''Course.' She liked being with the house, its quietness. Nobody shouting. Nor slapping. She liked the calm regular ways of the family, the professor in his coloured waistcoat always sitting at the harpsichord. The foreign coloured ladies upstairs practising their silent music. The Old Lady knitting. Toddlers in the bath. Always a fresh cake just out of the oven cooling on the kitchen table. She couldn't say all that. He'd think she was going soft. She said, 'I like the nice nosh your mum puts in the fridge. I get to fix myself good teas here.'

'Well, if I grow up, I don't want to have to look back and remember that I've had any part in your failure to get educated.'

'Yeah.'

'Because if you keep truanting, it's like you're stealing your own youth from yourself. If you truant, you won't get educated and then you'll be ignorant, impoverished, and socially disadvantaged for the rest of your life.'

'If. If. If. Don't you know no other word?'

'Indeed I do. If I let you come here during the daytime, I am conniving at your truancy. From now on, you may come round only after you've attended school.'

Stupid bossy perve, she thought. 'OK. Sure,' she said.

He said, 'And you're not to just wander about pretending you've been. You're going to have to tell me what you did, *every* day. I'll know if you're making it up.'

It wouldn't be too bad going in tomorrow and Friday. Just two days. It was half-term the week after.

'Rightio, Treasure.'

'And don't call me Treasure.'

'Only a joke.' The lollipop lady had once called her Treasure.

'It's not funny.'

'No humour, that's your problem.'

Walking back she remembered how Bedboy hadn't said, 'When I grow up,' but, 'If I grow up.'

That was weird. Everybody grows up. You can't help it. Sharon went on about it all the time. 'So I'll be glad when *you're* grown up and got out of my hair.' And, 'You're going to have to change your ways before you grow up, my girl!' And one time, 'I just pray on my knees that you'll begin to see some sense before you grow up.'

Becks said, 'Never seen *you* praying. Only time *you're* on your knees is when you've had too many Malibus.'

That made Sharon go ape.

Becks knew what she'd be when she grew up. Like Sharon. Poor, thick, angry, just as Bedboy warned, except he'd used his poncy words to say it. And Sharon was like *her* mum, except Nan wasn't so angry all the time. Maybe that wore off with time. Becks didn't want to be like either of them.

And perhaps poor Bedboy wasn't going to grow up at all. Weird wasn't in it. 'Have to give him a chance, won't I?' she thought. 'If he's on the way out, then I got to make up to him. I got to not be so mean. I got to do what he wants. Because he won't get a life like me.'

She reckoned she might get a couple of chances. Bedboy said everything came in sevens but he was wrong. Two was her full-house. Her Number One chance, most likely, was she'd end up like Sharon and Nan. But there was always this other teeny weeny itchy titchy chance in a million of Number Two. She'd end up rich and happy in a big house, with six nice babies, two dogs, a motorbike, and a kind hard-working husband like Nasreen's dad but without the big dark moustache, who'd go out to work for her. And by then Bedboy might be dead so she could never ask him round to tea.

Becks decided to make a vow on her life. Sharon was always vowing on her life. 'I vow on my life, as I live and breathe God's holy air, that I'll try not to grieve him.'

It felt really cool to make a vow like that.

On bad days, the stairwell of Block 4 smelt of dogs and men. It was a good day. The nasty odours had been doused with lemon disinfectant. The leaking bin-bags had been moved. The lift had been mended too.

But Sharon was in one of her peevey moods. She began yelling as soon as she opened the door. 'And just where the blooming heck you think you been? A slap round the head with a cold kipper's too good for you, and that's the truth.'

Becks ducked. Sharon shouted.

'Nothing but trouble is what you brought me with your deceitful ways and I had a letter about you from that school so I'll be before the magistrates if this goes on much longer and what d'you have to say about that?'

'I was gonna go tomorrow anyway. So you don't need to keep on shouting like I'm deaf.'

Sharon wasn't listening.

'You can get your own tea and put yourself to bed.'

'Had my tea,' Becks muttered. 'And a better one than you've ever given me.'

18 Amy and the Oven and the Robin's Eggs

Following the burial of their infant son, Miss Amy's parents distracted themselves from their intense grief by embarking on an extended European trip. From this, they eventually returned bearing gifts for their daughter, two important new items for Number Seven, a miniature harpsichord, and a miniature kitchen range, made of pressed tin and steel. The harpsichord had brass pedals, a brass key, and a marquetry wood inlay lid beneath which was hidden a wind-up musical box.

'See, Amy, it really plays!' said her mother. 'Tchaikovsky, *The Nutcracker Suite*. Wind it up and let's hear it now.'

It played the same tune over and over again without ever tiring.

The kitchen range, standing firm like a bath-tub on four curly feet, had two hot-plates on top, an oven inside, and had been forged, according to the imprint on the underside, in one of the great steelworks of the Ruhr. By placing a lighted night-light in the holder inside, it could really be made to work.

Amy recalled her delight at both these treasures, only later coming to reflect on the oddness of her parents' attempt to replace the loss of a brother and the three-month absence of themselves in such a way.

The range came with its set of dwarf-sized pots and pans. 'Mother, please may we try it?' Amy asked.

'No, dear, I rather think not, don't you? For matches and night-lights can be very dangerous in the hands of little girls. Why don't you use your imagination and *pretend* that you're cooking.'

Amy did not see much of her parents. Their grief was assuaged and now they were busy.

The next afternoon, Miss Amy and her nursemaid set out not to view the ducks but to raid a bird's nest. They returned with two small, beautifully pale, lightly freckled robin's eggs.

'And for Lordie's sake, don't tell your mother,' said the nursemaid.

Seventy years on Miss Winters reflected on changing values. Today, to remove two warm eggs from a wild bird's nest, even though leaving behind four, was an indictable offence.

But oh, how daintily delicious they had tasted, simmered gently in one of the tiny German pans, and then their tiny tops tapped open with a silver dolly spoon.

19 People who Gossip

So Becks went skulking along to school on Thursday. But she'd been away too long. The class had trotted miles ahead without waiting for her or any other stragglers. She was all left out and left behind. They'd moved on to doing a new kind of sums using the alphabet instead of numbers. It didn't make any sense, even when Nasreen tried to explain. And in Read-Aloud time, Mrs Whitton had finished the story of *The Little Princess* and was into a different one full of people Becks had never heard of.

'Don't keep telling me what's going on,' she snapped when Nasreen tried to tell her the early part of the story. 'You know I won't get it. I'm one of the dum-dums.'

Most peeving of all, at playtime the only thing they wanted to talk about was half-term and who'd been chosen to go on Country Week.

Nasreen said, 'I'm ever so sorry you won't be coming too. I did tell you, didn't I? You had to get your name down in time. But I'll bring you back something nice, promise.'

'Don't want nothing,' said Becks. 'I told you before, it's daft wanting to go to the naffing countryside to look at cow poo.'

Becks stuck it till dinner break then snuck off. She went up the Mall to hang about. In a kitchen gift shop she saw a shiny grater so small it looked like it was meant for grating doll's cheese. It had a label on saying 'Nutmeg', whatever that was. She snitched a handful of floor sweeties too, without anyone seeing. Half for Bedboy. Half for her.

The front door was opened by the woman in the blue overall who always smelt like old cigarette butts. She wasn't pleased to see Becks. But then she never was.

'Oh, it's you, is it. Well, he's out. And I'm just off home.'

'Out?' said Becks. How could he be out? He never went

out. He hadn't been out since she'd first found him.

'They're all out.'

Becks tried to push past.

'His mum's driven him up the hospital.'

'Hospital?'

'Got to see the consultant. Big chief doc. Got an appointment. All right, Miss Nosy? Anything else you want to know? Or are you going to hop it?'

'I gotta come in. I got something important for our little house.' She remembered her vow. 'For his little house.' She held up the grater.

'Soft, that's what he is. And his mum. Letting him play with girls' toys.'

'I gotta put this in just the right place. You know how fussy he is.'

'Very well, suit yourself. But I'm on my way.'

Becks went to the dining-room. She closed the door quietly behind her. The room looked even bleaker without him. He'd always been there. How could he go off without telling her about it?

She opened up the front of Number Seven. The rubber toddlers were quiet in their cot. With so many of them, they had to lie on top of each other. That was no way to treat little children. She slipped one of them into her pocket. He never took any notice of them. He'd probably never miss it. And even if he did, he'd still got the other five.

She put the shiny grater on the kitchen table so the Maid would see it when she came to get the dinner. They had a cooked meal every night. Sometimes they had a cooked midday meal too.

It must be hard work for the Maid looking after so many when most of them sat around doing nothing. Becks had a thought. She liked the Maid. She'd stay there and help. She'd get the range ready for doing some cooking. He'd shown her how it really worked. There was a stumpy candle he called a night-light you had to put inside.

There were real matches on the real mantelpiece. Becks fetched them. She opened the oven door of the range. But there wasn't any stumpy piece of night-light inside. Becks went to find the Maid. She was in the parlour, kneeling in front of the grate with the red bucket and the hearth-brush no bigger than a toothbrush. She'd cleaned out the grate. The family were all sitting on their chairs, staring at their painted fire with their painted faces.

On the drive across town to the Southern and General Hospital, Patrick's mother kept up a flow of banal chat. She observed what a mess the construction work for the new by-pass was making. Then she pointed out how attractive this year's hanging flower baskets, courtesy of the town council, were.

Patrick couldn't believe how she could let such insignificant thoughts occupy her at a time when they were on their way to see the consultant. But perhaps, even if they'd been taking him off to select his grave and make the funeral arrangements, she'd probably have managed to avoid any direct reference to it.

Patrick's father kept silent, no doubt thinking of all the essential things he ought to have been doing to oust the principal instead of sitting in his wife's car waiting for the lights to go green.

The nearest his mother got to referring to the purpose of the trip was to say, 'Nearly there,' as they turned in through the hospital gates and, 'Here we are then,' when she saw a sign saying, 'Out-Patients Parking This Way'.

They had to wait. Patrick knew they'd have to. It said so on his appointments card. You might as well not make a big deal out of it. You might as well sit there and wait patiently like everybody else, instead of twiddling your fingers and repeatedly glancing at your watch as his father did.

'You always have to wait in hospitals, Dad,' Patrick said as though he'd been in dozens of them. He thought that if his father had had to spend as many hours doing absolutely nothing as Patrick had over the past months, he wouldn't worry about fifteen minutes here or there.

Patrick found, to his surprise, that he quite liked sitting in the waiting-room, despite the pain in his legs. There was a curious companionship about being in it together. It was a clinic session specially for child patients with a variety of post-viral syndromes. One of them, a small girl of about Rebecca's age though much cleaner, was unable to walk even slowly like he did. She was wheeled about in a chair. In one way that made him feel good to know that he wasn't *that* bad. In another way, it depressed him.

The little girl didn't talk. He understood about that. Relating to other people used up so much energy, gave you a headache, made you tired. But she smiled. And she smiled.

It was weird. What had she got to smile about when she couldn't even walk? It made other people smile back at her, specially the nurses. Perhaps that was because she was so cute, with her yellow curls and big eyes, like a pretty doll, and her gentle pink smile.

Her hands lay limp on her lap. Everything had to be done for her.

Patrick's mother chatted merrily to the mother of the smiling child about hanging floral baskets and the construction of the by-pass. The other mother chatted back about her daughter's illness, how the little girl had, at the onset, been so weak she'd had to be admitted as an In-Patient and fed through tubes pushed down her nose. Just hearing about it made Patrick feel nauseous. He hoped he wouldn't get that bad.

20 Fire Fire Burning

What the people needed to cheer them up was a real fire that really worked. Becks took a match from the box and drew it along the side. Nothing much happened which was weird because that time Winston had the matches and all the stuff he wanted burning behind Block 2, it caught easy.

She tried again, pressing harder.

The brown match-head hissed as it flared up. It startled her. She dropped it. It went out even before it reached the floor. She had another go, striking more firmly. It caught light but she held it wrong so the flame jumped up and stung her finger. She dropped that one too.

Fourth time lucky, that's what Mrs Whitton once said when Becks was trying to sharpen a pencil with a lead that kept on breaking.

She held the match level so it wouldn't burn her finger. She put the neat flame to the shred of black crumpled paper that was meant to look like coal at the bottom of the painted grate. The paper caught.

For a moment, it looked exactly right, like a real coal fire warming the people in their smart re-papered parlour. They were smiling as usual and their eyes were bright.

But suddenly the flames were wrong for the room. They came jumping up like dangerous ginger cats. Over the wooden mantelpiece like scarlet tigers' tongues, reaching out for the clock-face that always said ten to nine at any time of day.

The fire teeth met the birthday cake candles on the mantelshelf, tasted wax, liked it, fed on it. The flames turned into leaping golden wolves, up to the lampshade. The parlour was ablaze with a miniature fire. The people sat staring. They didn't put up their hands to protect their hot faces. They didn't run for the door, didn't even care about the five toddlers so quiet in their cot upstairs. Becks watched. It was all happening too fast. Soon the lion flames would be clawing at the toddler's tiny toes.

This was nearly like a real fire with real smoke inside a real room. Somebody would have to do something about it. Soon they'd all be melting or frizzing or frying.

You had to have water for fire. A gushing hose-pipe, a spurting tap. A water cannon like the riot police used on the crowds. Becks collected some spit but not nearly enough. She heard someone whimpering. It was only herself.

There was half a glassful of apple juice on the chair by his bed. She grabbed it and flung it into the heart of the fire. It sizzled and made a smell of burning sweetness. There was still smoke.

At school, they had buckets of sand along the corridor. One of the boys once asked Mrs Whitton if the sand was so the firemen could make sand-castles and Mrs Whitton said sand smothers small fires. Becks must smother this fire. Blankets smothered you. Bedboy didn't have blankets. He had a big duvet. But that would ruin it to put it on the sizzling apple juice. Becks picked up the rug from the floor and draped it over the house. When the smoke stopped she pulled it off. She put it back on the floor and put the mug back on the chair.

The dolls watched her. That was their job, like Bedboy said, to see everything that happened but never to pass judgement.

The corridor outside the dining-room was quiet, just Bedboy's dog padding towards her wagging its tail and smiling. Her hands were weak and trembling. It seemed to take forever to get a grip on the front-door knob to turn it.

Out on The Avenues, she began to run and went on till she was through the park, past the Cash-and-Carry, into the industrial estate and out to the by-pass.

She didn't think about where she was going. She just had to get away before he came back and found out. Seeing the house would make him get one of those relapses. He'd get so bad that he'd stop breathing altogether and it'd be all her fault.

Pain began gnawing into her. It felt like there were rats inside her chest and piranhas in her head.

She had to get away.

21 Sitting on Small Chairs

The medical expert was young, female and Asian, with an unpronounceable surname. Her manner was milder than that of the jocular GP whom Patrick had never liked ever since he'd had a verruca removed by him. She addressed Patrick rather than his parents which made a decent change but she had no message of hope, no radical change of treatment to offer.

'You must expect some set-backs along the way but do not be downhearted by them,' she concluded. 'There are three essential things you require for recovery. Rest, rest, and rest. But combined with very gentle exercise, as you've been doing. Avoid stress. If it comes, learn not to react to it.'

Patrick thought of the things that worried him deep in the night. How could he learn not to worry about them?

'I believe you are an excellent scholar?'

Patrick nodded. He wondered if she'd known about the scholarship he'd won this time last year.

'And I expect you're getting behind with your studies now?'

'Yes,' said Patrick.

'Does this worry you or are you a happy-go-lucky type of chap?' Her language, Patrick thought, sounded colonial Raj. Perhaps she was older than she looked.

He said, 'It worries me a great deal. The others have all sat their Trials. I'm not sure about my subject choices now. You can't take chemistry if you never get into the lab. I keep changing my mind. I always used to know exactly what I thought or wanted. And if I have to think too much, I start to cry.'

'Emotional lability,' said the doctor nodding knowingly. 'Very often a symptom of central nervous system dysfunction. It will pass. But it might be some considerable time until you're well enough to resume full-time schooling. I believe you should consider applying to the Education Authority for Home Tuition. They're obliged by law to provide it. The medical secretary in reception will provide you with the necessary form.'

Patrick's father interrupted. 'You say, "some time". What d'you mean? How long is that?'

The beautiful, not so young, doctor was evasive. 'It varies so much from one individual to another. The shortest period of recovery among patients within my experience has been six weeks, but that was unusual in its brevity. The longest, again only in my own experience, seven years. And the average, thirty-seven months.'

'Thirty-seven months?' said Patrick. What an odd way of saying it. Did she mean three years and a bit more?

'You must remember that eventual recovery of at least forty per cent of your previous ability is the goal you are aiming for, though you may have to adapt your previous life-style.'

What life-style? Patrick wondered but did not say.

Not terminal but perpetual and forever. Not life-threatening but a lifetime. He couldn't stay like this for three whole years. And what was forty per cent of his life-style?

'At least twenty per cent of patients recover fully, very often the younger ones. I should like to see you again in three months so please make an appointment in Reception.'

And that was it. Dismissed. Time for the next patient. No medicine. No magic. No promises. Kind, but inconclusive. Patrick didn't feel he'd learned anything he didn't know already except that eighty per cent of people didn't fully recover ever. It was all a dread confirmation that this was going to be with him for a long time.

His mother went off to fetch the car while Patrick and his father sat at the Out-Patients' entrance. His father stood tapping the heel of one shoe against the toe of the other. Sitting upright was nearly as tiring as standing. Patrick saw a bench at the end of the passage. He went over and lay down along it. The pain, the fuzzy head, the heaving floor like sea, the weakness and urgent longing to be in a warm dark safe place. Nothing unusual. It was always like this, and it was going to go on being like this every time he extended himself in any way and often when he didn't.

Becks found she'd run all the way back to Wellend. She was on her way to school. The only chance of escape. Get hold of Mrs Whitton. If she hadn't gone home yet.

She passed the chippy where the fish-clock in the window said it was five to four, *always time for a fine fish tea*. She was going to be too late. They'd all be gone home by now. But maybe the chippy clock was fast?

The playground was empty. Very quiet. No kids, no staff, no nattering nans. School was done for the day. If Mrs Whitton had gone, Becks might as well crawl into a corner and die like a poisoned rat.

She belted round to the side where the door was propped open with a rubbish bin. That meant the lollipop lady was still here sweeping out the corridors. And if she was still here, then Mrs Whitton was still here too because they were friends. You weren't meant to come in by the side door. It was a fire door, for Emergencies. This was one of them. She'd set fire to a house and she was on the run.

Mrs Whitton was in the Infants' room, sorting books in their Reading Corner. She was eating a milk chocolate wafer. That surprised Becks because Mrs Whitton was always saying she didn't like people with chocolate in their hands turning the pages of the books.

Then she put on her stern look.

'Well, well,' she said when Becks explained she'd changed her mind and wanted to come on Country Week after all. 'You've left it far too late for this about-turn,' said Mrs Whitton. 'But I suppose you better tell me all about it.'

Mrs Whitton sighed and sat down at one of the Infants' desks. It was weird seeing a fully grown teacher trying to lower herself on to a little red chair which didn't fit.

It was like that time Becks tried to get Wooden Woman to

come into the kitchen to join in the birthday tea for the toddlers. Wooden Woman was too tall. Becks had to let her stand in the hall and have her food handed to her through the door. She got the plate of fancy coloured cakes to make up for being outside.

Mrs Whitton pulled out another tiny chair for Becks. It was painted blue like the sky. Becks remembered how simple things were when you were in Infants.

'So what's made you change your mind, all of a sudden?'

'Dunno really.' Becks stared down at Mrs Whitton's shoes. They were brown and polished with a neat buckle across the toes. Becks wished Sharon would wear nice ones like that.

'Something must have. Last week you were adamant that nothing would induce you to take part in this wonderful opportunity.'

Becks didn't know what adamant meant. She guessed it was to do with Mrs Whitton being annoyed.

'I know things aren't always easy for you at home, are they? Has something happened?'

'No.'

'If you'd like to tell me about it, whatever it is, I will listen. And you have my confidence.'

Becks knew that this was it. The moment she'd been needing. A person actually asking to hear everything she needed to say. This was the time to get rid of the secret. Nothing would be worse than hanging on to it in the darkness of her heart where it scratched against the inside of her chest every time she breathed.

'It's like this,' she began. But the moment slipped into silence. There weren't any words to describe any of the things she had to say.

'As you know, Rebecca, I was disappointed. I told you how much I wanted you to join in Country Week. Yours was one of the very first names put forward to the selection panel. Someone who'd really benefit from the experience. All the places have been allocated now. I'm sorry, Rebecca. But there it is.'

Becks stared at the floor and gulped. A chance of escape disappeared down a crack in the classroom floorboards.

'At least it'll be a useful lesson for you. About making sensible decisions at the right moment. And not thinking you can hang on till the last minute and keep everyone guessing.'

'Don't care,' was all Becks could say. 'I never cared.'

'I know,' said Mrs Whitton. 'That's the trouble. It seems you can never let yourself care about anything.'

The scratching inside the cage of Becks's chest was pressing outwards like a thorny bush. She felt her shoulders heaving as though she was being choked to death from the inside.

Mrs Whitton took a tissue out of a packet in her handbag. 'Here, have this,' she said.

'I ain't crying, if that's what you think. I just got something stuck in my neck what was choking me.' Becks blew her nose.

Mrs Whitton said, 'By now, as I said, all the places are allocated. However, Steve's mother rang school this morning. It's probably nothing serious but he was a bit poorly with a sore throat so he might have to pull out.'

The lollipop lady suddenly barged into the classroom with her noisy bucket and jangling bunch of keys.

'Sorry to intrude. Didn't think you was still on the premises,' she said. 'I've to lock up now.'

'That's all right, Annie,' said Mrs Whitton. 'We're just on our way.'

Becks was surprised. She'd never thought of the lollipop lady having a name.

Mrs Whitton said, 'So you trot along home like a good girl and we'll see what the morrow brings. All right?'

22 Stealing from Yourself

'Complete waste of time,' Patrick's father said to Patrick's mother when they were in the car and back on the ring road.

'D'you think so?' said Patrick's mother. 'As a matter of fact, I found it rather reassuring to see that he's nowhere near as bad as that poor little girl.'

'Why couldn't she *cure* him, or at least admit she didn't know how?'

'I thought she was refreshingly honest, and most helpful,' said Patrick's mother. 'A really nice woman.'

Patrick's father grunted, then said, 'You do remember I've got a meeting at half past. Drop me off at the City Cross.'

Patrick's mother said, 'You know I can't. There's a diversion all round there with the road works.'

Patrick's head hurt. He wanted to yell at them both to stop bickering.

He said, 'You're mad, both of you. Crazy. It's like nothing real's ever going to touch you, isn't it? Instead of contradicting each other, why don't you yell and scream and shout and say that this is the worst thing that's ever, ever happened to you? To any of us? Why don't you do something as though you really cared? If it was *my* only child who was incapacitated I know I wouldn't be able to bear it. I'd just give up.'

'Of course we can't give up,' said his father over his shoulder, as though surprised that Patrick was still there on the rear seat behind him.

'We have to be strong,' agreed his mother. 'For your sake.'

'Pretending that this isn't the worst thing that's ever happened isn't strong. It's stupid. Why won't you admit it's dreadful? You keep being cheerful. You keep saying I'll be better soon. It's not true. It makes me feel it's my *fault* I'm not recovering, as though I asked for this virus to invade me.'

That did the trick. It was as though Patrick had finally managed to trigger the alarm button. His mother swerved left into the bus lane so that the truck on her tail nearly rammed into the back of them. She dropped her head on to the steering wheel and began to whimper.

'You're right, you're right. I can't bear it, I can't bear it. Can't, can't,' she seemed to be saying.

Patrick's father took off his glasses and sat motionless. He seemed incapable of offering solace to Patrick's mother. She sobbed while he sat like a weeping rock.

Patrick had no strength left. He wanted to lie down on the back seat with the rug over his head. Instead, he pulled himself upright, leaned forward and put his arms round both of them.

He said, 'It's going to be all right. You heard her. Three years. I've done half a year already. By the time I'm eighteen—'

'Eighteen!' his mother gasped.

'If I haven't taken any exams by then, it still won't be too late to start.'

Patrick comforted them both. He felt worse, yet better as well. They were all in it together. He noted that his father wept in a strange way, like a little boy, with lots of sniffing but not much noise. It made Patrick feel affectionate towards him. He looked so vulnerable.

As for his mother, he hadn't realized that she had so much crying inside her trying to get out.

'I don't want you to give up on me, Mum. I need you. You know it. I do. To be there. I need both of you.' He was astonished to hear himself say so much. 'I love you, Mum.'

Patrick's mother blew her nose. 'It's been unbearable watching your youth, your whole childhood, being stolen from you like this.'

Patrick remembered saying much the same thing to Rebecca, accusing her of stealing her youth from herself. And that was just what he'd been doing too. A disease can't steal. It was how you responded to it that counted.

* * *

Becks told Sharon, 'I been chosen special to go on Country Week. And you have to take them in the ten pounds.'

That part was true enough. That was the way they did all the treats at school. They set up something good, told you it was free, then made parents pay a contribution towards the costs.

'Money, money, money, that's all you ever think of,' snapped Sharon.

'Oh, come on. It's only ten quid.'

'Only?' said Sharon. 'Just so you can hop off and have a nice leisure break while I slave away here. I think Madam better have another think about her holiday.'

'It's not much to pay for getting rid of me. I'd pay ten quid to be rid of *you* for a week.'

Becks knew, too late, she shouldn't have said it. She ducked but not in time to avoid a slap round the head.

'Bit less of the cheek wouldn't do you any harm. Now keep quiet because it's building up to Bud and Karen's big day. The engagement.' Sharon turned up the volume on the telly. 'And I want to follow without your naffing chatter.'

Becks rubbed her ear. It didn't hurt as much as the pain inside her but she still hated being hit. Not all children got slapped. Bedboy had never been hit by an adult in his whole life, or so he said. Nobody in Number Seven ever hit either. The rubber toddlers just rolled and laughed and gurgled their happy days away in a life without fear. Even the tin dog was peaceful, never growled, never tried to bite.

Then, with a return of the terrible pain, Becks remembered that that was how it used to be at Number Seven, all quiet and contented. That was before she'd moved in and done that terrible thing, setting fire to them, trying to choke them all to death.

In the darkness, Becks spoke to the orphan toddler who lived under her pillow. She called her Annie after the lollipop lady. Just because she had no arms, didn't mean she had to have no name. She told her how she didn't want poorly Steve to suffer too much, not as much as Bedboy, but she did hope that his sore throat wouldn't get better *too* quickly. If he could stay poorly for just another couple of days, he wouldn't be well enough for Country Week.

In the newspaper, Miss Winters read the obituary of a colleague with whom she had worked forty years before.

'So all my friends are dead or dying and the stage is fast becoming empty. My time soon.'

But had she left everything in order? Had she made arrangements so she'd be no bother to anybody after she was gone? Who was she leaving her things to? Had she written her will?

Oh dear, it was becoming difficult to remember everything that had to be remembered.

Marmalade sat expectantly by the larder door. His expression suggested that he was waiting to be fed.

But surely, thought Miss Winters, I have already fed him? Or have I? Better not let him see that I can't remember. Better feed him again, just in case, for an empty sack never stands upright.

At school, Nasreen told Becks that Steve still had a sore throat. And Mrs Whitton told her it was tonsillitis and he was on antibiotics.

'So it looks like this is your lucky break,' she said.

Becks nodded. But she couldn't smile for she wasn't away yet. She said, 'I ain't got the money. I'll be fetching it at dinner time,' even though she knew that Sharon was never going to cough up. She'd have to nick it. Fifty pee was easy enough. But ten quid?

Mrs Whitton's handbag was over on the book-shelf in Reading Corner and her back was turned. Becks could wander over, pick a book off the shelf, dip in her hand.

'Money, dear?' said Mrs Whitton. She was filling in a form with Becks' name at the top. 'By the way, dear, you'll have to get your mother to sign the consent form this evening. For the insurance.'

110

'That money what everybody has to bring. My mum hasn't got none. I already asked.'

'Oh that. I dare say we can fiddle it some way.'

Mrs Whitton do a fiddle? 'How d'you mean, Miss?'

'School contingency fund. I'm sure the Head'll let us have something from there if we ask nicely.'

Mrs Whitton was in a right mivvy mood. So was the Head. So was Sharon who signed the consent form without giving Becks any grief.

'Frankly, I'll be glad to see the back of you. Give me a bit of peace and quiet.' She handed Becks a plastic carrier. Inside was a new toothbrush, a face flannel, and a big bar of soap still in its wrapper.

'You bought them special,' said Becks, surprised.

'That's for your little holiday. You mind you wash yourself all over. So these people'll know you been properly brought up.'

Sharon had never told her to wash all over before. But then Becks had never before been away with strangers.

'And you behave too. I don't want to hear no tales of you playing up.'

She gave Becks three packets of crisps for her dinner on the journey, a peck on the cheek, and seventy-five pence spending money. Then she stood at the kitchen window looking out so that when Becks reached the ground floor, Sharon was still up there waving through the glass. The only thing Sharon didn't do was walk Becks along to school and wave her off in the coach like all the other mothers.

PART FOUR
Half-term and After That

23 The Fading Dye of Leaves

The uppermost branches of the tall and stately plane trees lining The Avenues moved gently in the breeze. Although Marmalade was probably not able to register and delight in the elegance of their movements, Miss Winters was.

What a joy it was to have one's very own armchair, to be at liberty to sit near to one's window, with a rose-bush and waving trees conveniently situated immediately beyond. And beyond that, a quiet street with enough spasmodic come and go to provide interest.

There had been something troubling her earlier. But now she couldn't remember what it was so it could not have been very important.

The milk float trundled silently down the centre of the road. Next, a learner-driver proceeded cautiously forward into Miss Amy Winters' view and came to practise the reversing procedures alongside the kerb immediately outside Miss Amy Winters' window. Marmalade perked up and twitched one ear with interest.

All this within sight.

So much to be thankful for.

What a secure and contented childhood had been provided for her. What a useful education and training she had been given. What a rich and full life it had been. And, thereafter, what a pleasant retirement it still was.

She remembered how there had been roses at Number Seven, a gift from her nursemaid one Christmas. Two miniature flower-pots made of real earthenware were planted with tiny wire-stemmed bushes stuck all over with fabric leaves and flowers. The blooms had been scarlet, the leaves a vivid lime green.

They had seemed so marvellously realistic when she was a child. Only now did she realize how those crude colourings had been too bright. Burnished gold was the colour of real rose leaves. Over the years, the dyes had faded until the green leaves and scarlet petals became a similar brownish sepia colour, though of course they could never wither and drop like real leaves and blooms.

Miss Winters patted yesterday's newspaper still folded neatly upon her lap. She would read it, not now but later, to learn of the world's goings-on, see if there were any good obituaries. Although past it, she was not out of it.

'Am I, puss?' she said.

Everything about the trip should have been ace. She knew in her mind it was. Perfect as heaven. She could see it with her eyes. Yummy picnics on the grass. The giggling baby. Blue bright sky. Furriness of lambs.

She couldn't feel any of it.

'Are you very homesick, you poor dear?' the mother at the cottage asked. 'We could pop down to the phone box and give your mum a ring tonight if it would help?'

'She ain't got no phone neither,' said Becks.

The girls of the family helped Becks send a postcard. Miriam and Laura chose a view of stone cottages and flower-filled fields, just like where they lived. They helped her write the message. They took her to the post office on the edge of the village green.

Having a good time. Went to Shire Horse Centre today. And I helped to feed baby cows. I miss you. See you next week. Love from Becks, was what they helped her write.

But it wasn't Sharon she wanted to send a message to. It was Bedboy. Sorry, sorry, sorry, she wanted to say. And then all over again. Sorry, sorry, sorry.

But just writing sorry, sorry, sorry on a picture postcard was never going to put it right.

In the evening she felt the pain gnaw deeper. It was a hungry guard dog. She fell asleep in the cosy low room under the thatch that she shared with two of the girls. Tired with all the fresh air, she told herself that by morning, it would all be hot diggety dog again. She woke to another sunny day, weighed down by the sick dread.

Miss Winters was feeling peculiar, not unwell but distinctly unusual. This was the second day in succession that she was unable to attempt her regular trot along to the park. Better to wear out than to rust out, she used to say. Yet here she was sitting in the armchair instead of out walking, wearing neither shoes nor stockings, wondering what strangeness might be going on.

Marmalade settled uneasily amongst the knick-knacks upon the occasional table, no longer observing clouds, now closely observing his servant. He too wished to know what on earth was going on. The instant she should remember to rise and move towards the kitchen to prepare his food he would be ready to eat.

Each of them from Wellend was put with a separate family. They met up every day in a place they called the Village Hall beside the field they called the Recreation Ground. The family Becks got was really ginger, everyone said, especially poor Tom who'd got put with a stonky old couple in a smelly bungalow full of budgies.

Becks' lot had a farm, only they called it a smallholding. There was five children, Miriam and Laura, Abbie, Willum, and the giggling baby, Ruth. Their cottage didn't look like the houses in Becks' mind, yet once you were part of it, you could feel how the important things were the same. Windows always open. Chimneys with blue wood-smoke coming out the top. Front door, which wasn't really a front door but a kitchen door on the side, always a bit open so people and cats and dogs could wander in and out. Sometimes the hens walked in too, though they weren't supposed to.

The people were welcoming but didn't make a fuss about it, just like the people at Number Seven. The big girls had special jobs to do about the place, but they didn't mind when Becks didn't want to join in picking vegetables, but sat on the grass watching.

With her eyes and her ears, Becks knew that these were kind people, doing everything to help her have a perfect week.

Miss Amy Winters remained in the armchair. She was confused but surely not unwell? Yet she could not stand. She could not move her own limbs. Her hands were so heavy. It was all highly irregular. But not to worry. What's done cannot be undone.

There was just one time when all the fear inside was washed away. It was the day before the end. They were going to the seaside.

Miriam was astonished when she found out that Becks had never seen the sea.

'Nope,' said Becks. 'But I seen it on the telly. I know what it looks like.'

'That's not the same. On the telly, you can't smell it.'

'Or taste it,' said Laura.

'Or feel the sand and the rocks spiking your feet.'

'The poor little scrappet,' Becks heard the smallholding mother say to the smallholding father. 'She's tense all the time. She doesn't know how to relax.'

Becks was surprised. She never thought of herself as small. She thought she was big.

'It can't be right,' said the smallholding mother. 'Bringing them up in blocks like that with no grass.'

Becks didn't like hearing them talk about things they didn't understand.

They drove to the coast in the van that the smallholding father used on other days for transporting lambs. At the seaside, there was a blustering wind. Great waves like elephants heaved up the beach.

Becks heard herself laughing above the noise as they ran

down the wet sand to chase the wild water before it turned and chased them back.

Little Abbie, her skirt tucked into her knickers, was knocked over by a huge roller. She went down under the white steaming foam. She bobbed up, grinning, scrambled to her feet. She was drenched and didn't even cry. For a three year old, she was cool.

Becks said, by mistake, 'Wish I could stay here forever.' In the excitement of Abbie nearly drowning, and the noise of the water, nobody heard.

The father carried Abbie up the shingle and the mother wrapped her in a towel. Becks began to tremble.

There was that tightness in her chest. She didn't know what it was. It spread up her neck. She felt she was drowning. Her shoulders began heaving as though she was going to be sick. She gasped for breath even though it wasn't her who'd nearly drowned.

She didn't ever cry. It wasn't her style. She hadn't done it for years. But here she was in front of these strangers, starting to weep.

The mother held her and tried to comfort her but Becks couldn't find any of the words that had to be let out to explain.

The angry yowling issuing from the letter-box drew the postman's attention to the fact that all was not well behind Miss Amy Winters' front door. It sounded like a cross and hungry cat. He alerted the neighbours on one side, who went across to the neighbours on the other side who kept a spare key to Miss Winters' home.

As soon as the door was opened, Marmalade slithered like an eel out between the intruders' legs before any of them even noticed him leave.

He slunk off down The Avenues, sniffing at every gateway, cautious yet eager to find a decent place to live.

* * *

119

The parents put into immediate effect some long-term planning for Patrick's welfare. They had the dining-room walls repainted. Patrick chose the colour from a chart. It was called *Spanish Sun*. They had new curtains made up in glowing Mediterranean colours. Patrick's father pruned back the tired and straggling shrubs and planted a eucalyptus tree with flickering blue leaves. Patrick's mother fetched down his best posters from his old bedroom and put them on the dining-room walls. It didn't look so much like a dining-room any more. It looked like a student den.

'It's quite good now, isn't it?' Patrick said. 'I'm really going to like being in here.'

'Me too,' said his father. He was crouched on the floor busily sandpapering the smoked banisters of Number Seven for he had taken on the job of cleaning the whole thing up. He actually seemed to be enjoying it too.

'It's most satisfying,' he said. 'You can redecorate a whole room in less than an hour when the ceiling's only ten inches high.'

24 Home Again, Jiggety Jog

On the coach ride back to Wellend, Becks sat next to Nasreen. Nasreen gossiped cheerily like some little naffin. She told Becks every detail of her week, every sheep she'd stroked, every blade of grass she'd seen, every cow-pat she'd not stepped in.

'They were nice, my Mr and Mrs Hawthorn, but I won't half be glad to get home to my mum for a proper meal. It was potatoes, potatoes every time. They just lived on them.'

Becks said, 'Nazz, if you was on your way back home, like now, and you'd done something bad a long time ago, what would you do?'

'How d'you mean? How wrong? Like bunking off? Don't fret yourself. Everybody knows you do it.'

Becks shook her head. 'No, something really bad.'

'Nicking stuff? Becks, most people know it's you does that too. Well, no, not most people. More like quite a few. Though I'd never tell my mum on you, honest, Becks, I wouldn't.'

'Wouldn't mind if you did. Anyway, it's nothing like nicking.'

'Worse than that? Like Grievous Bodily Harm?' Nasreen was beginning to look shocked and interested.

Becks felt Nasreen putting an arm round her. 'Oh, Becks. This is really a very terrible thing. You *must* tell somebody. A grown-up friend who can help you.'

'Haven't got any friends. Well, I did have one, but he's the one who's mixed up with this.'

'He's done it too?'

'No, he hasn't done nothing. He can't. It's more like he's the one I done that bad thing to.'

Nasreen said, 'Whatever it was, if it was me, I'd tell my mother.'

'Can't. You know what my mum's like,' Becks muttered.

'You must find somebody. What about a holy man, a priest? That's what they're for. They're never allowed to grass on you. Even if you killed someone. Oh, Becks, it's not that, is it?'

Becks thought of five rubber toddlers, the Maid, the Old Lady, Wooden Woman, the twelve Indian musicians, and all of them, probably blackened, melted and dead.

It was a bit like she'd murdered them.

'Sort of.'

Nasreen gasped.

Miss Amy Winters smiled when the nurses in Admissions told her that she had had a stroke.

'Thank you so very much,' she replied with a gracious nod of her head. 'All good things come to those who wait.'

'You're in the Western Infirmary, Amy. The hospital. We're taking care of you here. You're going to be all right,' they told her. 'You'll soon be better.'

'Thank you,' said Miss Winters. 'So very much.' She wondered why the stranger was calling her by her first name. No one ever called her Amy these days. Even as a child it was Miss Amy.

'Oh,' they said, whoever they were, 'I don't think she can hear us.'

Miss Amy Winters could hear. And she knew how wrong they were. She was not going to get better. She was on her way to meet her Maker.

'Is there anyone we can contact for you, Amy? Miss Winters? Any family? She must have *some* next-of-kin, surely. Everybody has somebody. Miss Winters, can you hear?'

'Perfectly, thank you, dear. I'm not deaf.'

Miss Amy Winters thought how that old mog, whatever his name was, was her real family, her next-of-kin. You couldn't count a second cousin's son who went to Australia. Only met him half a dozen times. Hardly knew him.

122

But that cat, a tough kitty he was. Someone would feed him, take care of him, he'd make sure of it.

And the house where she had spent her childhood, that was a worry. Who would take care of it now? Had she made arrangements or not? She simply could not remember, though she thought there was a child involved. Perhaps it was the cousin's son's daughter. That must be it.

'We're just going to make you comfortable now, Amy, Miss Winters,' they said.

But I *am* comfortable, Miss Amy Winters thought.

Meanwhile, Marmalade spent a cold uncomfortable time under a parked car. Later, he sniffed his way down The Avenues till he successfully sidled in through an open window, rubbed his back against a chair leg and made himself at home in a new residence.

Miss Amy Winters was no longer distressed and uncertain. She was relaxed and calm. The slight confusion of the previous days faded and clarity took its place, like the long hard night fading and the softer light of dawn taking over. Time could indeed work many wonders.

They kept asking her if she knew where she was, the silly young geese. She knew exactly where she was. She was in the four-poster, tucked warm, safe, snug beneath the cosy square of red felted wool she had snipped from the corner of her nursemaid's jacket to make a nice little blanket.

The Old Lady was busy today, playing nurse, wearing the dainty white apron and the cap with the red cross crayoned on the front. Miss Amy Winters had distinctly heard her busying about the room, taking care of her patients, and now she sat still on the Windsor-backed chair watching over her.

In the grate flickered the painted flames of the pretence fire.

'A fire on a summer evening is such a simple luxury,' said Miss Amy Winters.

The Old Lady smiled her serenely reassuring smile and continued to keep watch, to see what she saw and make no comment.

Cotton curtains fluttered at the open windows. From the bed, Amy sensed the security, the reassurance, the cheerful babble and bustle of family life. The six babies romped in their nursery upstairs while, downstairs in the smoky parlour, the professor played his harpsichord, filling the house with the cheerful tinkle of Tchaikovsky's *Nutcracker Suite*, time after time, always missing those last three notes. The tin dog scratched beneath the kitchen table. The Maid prepared the tea. Wooden Woman stood on the landing, the only place in the whole house where her tall stiff body fitted, and the Indian musical troupe played silently on.

Miss Amy Winters sighed with deep contentment and closed her eyes. Surrounded by such love, such companionship, she was not lonely and she would never be lonely again.

'A cherry year, a merry year, a plum year, a dumb year,' she said though the nurse beside her could not make out the exact words.

25 Seven Times Number Seven

Becks didn't take Nasreen's advice. Instead, she scurried silently to school, head down, hood up, even though it was so sunny. Any day someone out looking for her was going to spot her, pounce, and drag her off to her accusation and trial. Becks tried to tell herself she was safe now. She'd never told him her address. He'd never be able to find her up here.

In dinner break she stayed close to the wall on the shadowy side. After school, she darted home, hood up, eyes down. Through the long dreamy evenings of summer, when the other kids played out till late on the drying yellow grass amongst the dog dirt and crisp packets, she stayed in.

Sharon said it was a miracle. 'All my prayers answered!' She gave Becks fifty pence. 'I knew you'd see sense in the end.'

Sharon had a new job, not much of a one, as she moaned to Becks, but every little helped.

'Specially with all that fancy uniform you'll be begging me for when you go up to secondary.'

She helped out in Nasreen's uncle's All-Nite All-Rite Stores. It was Mrs Ahmed who mentioned to Becks to tell her mum they were needing someone extra. Becks told Sharon she could say a thank you to Mrs Ahmed when she saw her.

'You joking or what? I don't owe nothing to no one,' said Sharon.

When I grow up, Becks told Annie with no arms, I'm going to try to be good and become a lollipop lady and help other people.

All the while that Miss Winters lay dying, the little house called Number Seven that was inside a larger house which was on The Avenues, waited in suspense, keeping so still it seemed to be holding its breath. There was not the faintest creak of plywood warping, nor the lightest flutter of a draught ruffling the skimpy curtains which Becks had stitched and which smoke had then stained to a sepia brown, not a whisper from a rubber child with melted rubber feet, not a single simple snore from a sleeping tin dog.

Far away on the other side of town, Amy Winters was safe with the nice young nurses. And there, in their intensive care, she passed peacefully away. And from within, from the little house inside the big house on The Avenues, seemed to come a collective sigh of relief that the dying was done.

The First Owner is dead. Long live the New.

An unexpected little breeze caused the dining-room door to the big house to slam which shook the floorboards, though only very slightly. The brief tremble jolted the little house back into its quiet rhythm.

The mechanism inside the professor's harpsichord, overwound by Becks till the coiled spring was tight as a granny-knot, was released and played the first three bars from the *Nutcracker Suite* all by itself without the professor even having to lift his hands. The dog scrabbled briefly and then settled down to sleep. The people, eyes bright, were alert and waiting. They would be ready, however long it took until they reached their new owner.

There was a letter for Becks. Flat 43 never got letters, just Sharon's catalogues and brown bills. So she grabbed it first and opened it.

'What's all this then?' She skimmed through it to the end. 'Oooh, you sly little fox, you. It's from a boy. You never told me you had no boyfriend. Bit young for that, aren't you?'

'Give it!' Becks said. She snatched it back so that it tore.

'Some country duffhead you met on your holiday, is it?'

'No.'

He might have been a friend, but never a boyfriend.

It was a long letter, now with a tear down the middle, in scrawly handwriting which Becks couldn't read.

She wasn't going to let Sharon get another peek. She took it to Annie, the lollipop lady, to read for her.

Dear Rebecca,
This missive concerns No 7. Something rather unfortunate occurred some time back and, considering all the work you put in, I felt you ought to know.

'No seven,' said the lollipop lady. 'What's that mean?'
'Number Seven,' said Becks. 'It's a mystical number. To do with stars and wonders of the world and boots and stuff.'
'Sounds mysterious. Conjuring trick, is it?'
'Yeah, sort of,' said Becks. She didn't want the lollipop lady to talk about the letter, just to read it.

You certainly are elusive. It was exceedingly difficult tracking you down till my mother worked out which school you probably go to. They wouldn't give us your address. But the secretary said they'd forward my letter.

About No. 7, it seems that Mrs Murphy, whom you may remember, dropped some burning ash on to it. My mother says there's no other explanation, unless of course it was that glue we used. In fact, apart from the parlour, it wasn't too badly damaged, just a bit smoked and my father put most of it to right, in time.

The main problem has been the old lady to whom it formerly belonged. It turned out she's gone and died. She was quite old. But my mother was somewhat shocked when she heard about it. She'd seen her only the week before.

Anyway, the point is that I was hoping we could hang on to it, in spite of the fire, for quite a while. However, it transpires that the old lady bequeathed all her possessions to some relation in Australia. There's nothing we can do to prevent it leaving. Some removals

127

men have already been round to measure up for the case. So I'm afraid that's the end of that. I hope you won't be too upset.

I'd like to say, if it's not too forward, that I missed your company no end. It would be great if you ever decided to call round again, only if you feel like it, of course. Without No. 7 it probably wouldn't be so interesting for you.

There's a Home Tutor comes in once a day to teach me. He's a gas. Otherwise, everything's the same. And I'd always welcome a visit.

Yours, as ever,

Patrick L. Chambers

Becks wondered if she'd ever dare go and see him. And if she did, if she'd tell him what really happened.

D'you want to know something, Bedboy, it was me done it, she could say.

And he'd probably say, Hm, yes. Rather thought so. Well, please don't do it again.

The rumour of a move to Australia reached the inhabitants of Number Seven, waiting in the darkness inside the packing case inside the airfreight hangar near the loading bay. Australia was upside-down on the other side of the globe. A long way to travel for a new owner, yet in a world where nothing, least of all time, was to scale, nothing was too far, nothing too surprising.

Wooden Woman's stern gaze indicated that they would all find out what was going to happen to them next when it came about and not before.

At the end of the second week of secondary school term, Becks plucked up courage to make her way back to The

Avenues. She bunked off netball but that was no big deal. Lots of girls did.

Patrick's mother came to the front door. 'Oh, hello, dear,' she said kindly. 'Do come in. He'll be most awfully pleased to see you.'

He was in the same room though the bed was in a different place, over near the window. He had a new duvet cover patterned with sunflowers.

Becks said, 'You've changed it all about.'

The whole room was brighter, more colourful. There were big cushions on the floor and posters on the walls.

He said, 'Mum and Dad redid it for me.'

She said, 'Sorry I couldn't bring you nothing. Didn't get the time. I go to secondary school now.'

'So I see. Nice uniform.'

'We do French.'

'That's good, specially if you ever go travelling.'

'And CDT, you know, woodworking and stuff. Most people are making stupid spice-racks. I'm building a house, just a little one. It's for kids to play with.' That was the nearest she came to speaking of Number Seven. She edged towards the door.

'Well, gotta flit now. Got my homework to see to.'

'Come again, if you can, any time.'

She shrugged. 'Maybe. It all depends.'